Stephen

SAMUEL'S PRIDE SERIES   BOOK 4

KATHI S. BARTON

This is a work of fiction. Names, characters, places, and incidents are products of the author's imagination or are used fictitiously and are not to be construed as real. Any resemblance to actual events, locations, organizations, or person, living or dead, is entirely coincidental.

WCP

World Castle Publishing, LLC
Pensacola, Florida

Copyright © Kathi S. Barton 2014
Print ISBN: 9781629891620
eBook ISBN: 9781629891637
First Edition World Castle Publishing, LLC, September 17, 2014
http://www.worldcastlepublishing.com

Licensing Notes

Cover: Karen Fuller
Photos: Shutterstock
Editor: Eric Johnston
Editor: Maxine Bringenberg

Dedication

To my own Velvet December. Thank you. From the bottom of my heart I thank you for giving my villain life! She is, in a word, a bitch. I hope you enjoy Velvet as much as I did writing about her.

Chapter 1

The meeting could have gone better, he supposed, but Stephen wasn't in the mood to be ordered about at this stage of his life. Grinning, he thought of the look on Jared's face when he'd told him how old he really was. And he knew that Samuel hadn't helped a great deal with the situation either.

"You think you have powers that the rest of us don't? Let me tell you, buddy, I've been around for over three thousand years, and I can do things you only can dream about." Stephen had looked at the man and then at his friend, Samuel, before continuing. The kid just thought he was all that, didn't he?

"You gonna tell him or can I?" Stephen shrugged at Samuel as if he didn't care who told the idiot. Samuel looked as if he might have enjoyed telling the little pisser more than Stephen would anyway. Stephen was sure it would be a good deal safer for the idiot. "Stephen isn't just old, you moronic dick. He's been around over twice your lifetime."

"There is no way. If that were true, he'd be in charge of all vampires." Jared looked at Stephen then back at Samuel before he continued. "You're lying."

"I don't lie. And for the record, he was asked...no, he was begged...to watch over all you little piss ants, but he declined. For whatever reason, he thought he'd kill the lot of you before he got things the way he wanted." Samuel laughed. "I can see now why he didn't want the job. I might kill you myself and be done with it."

Jared had hissed at Samuel, but before his friend could react, Stephen had reached across the table and grabbed Jared around the throat. And when he let a little of his beast go, Jared stopped struggling.

"This is how this is going to go. You can either pick door one or door two. It matters little to me. Understand?" Stephen wanted to snap Jared's neck but waited while the man nodded as best he could. "Good. You're going to go out of this diner and never return. Your orders to me, any of them, will be sent to me via email or a messenger. Either way is fine by me. Doesn't mean I'll heed them, but you can send them. Or—and this is the one that I'd like to have you pick—you can simply open that mouth of yours again and I will tear your throat out."

Stephen let him go, and Jared opened his mouth. Just as he was reaching for him to kill him, Samuel interceded on Jared's part. "Don't," was all he said, and Jared looked at him. Then when he stood up and walked toward the door, Stephen looked at Samuel.

"I would rather have killed him. He's going to be a pain in my ass." Samuel nodded. "But you still saved him. Why?"

"Because, my dear friend, had you killed him as we both wanted you to do, you would have been forced to replace him. Do you really want to be the Master of all Vampires?" Stephen shuddered, and Samuel laughed as he continued. "Right. I didn't think so. And because I saved you a lifetime of servitude, you can buy me breakfast."

That had been over an hour ago. And now he sat at the counter waiting for…well, he had no idea, but he still waited. When Joann came toward him with a cup he started to tell her no, but she sat it in front of him and he could smell the warm blood.

"Thought you could use this about now." He nodded, not sure what to say to her. He knew that she was a wolf, but had no idea how she knew what he was. "Samuel. He called just now and said that you were in need of something to sustain you. Took me a minute to figure out what he meant. Then he said microwave it for only fifteen seconds."

"Thank you." She nodded and turned toward the door when the little bell over it rang. The child…no, that wasn't right. The woman standing there looked like she'd crawled from a deep hole. The hat she had on obscured any hint as to what color her hair might be, or even if she had any. Her pale skin made him think it was that way naturally rather than from her predicament, whatever that might be. For some reason he knew she was homeless because she was hiding rather than from a monetary situation. Before he could ascertain why she looked so dirty yet her face and hands were so clean, Joann spoke.

"You know you can't come in here on Mondays. He's in the back. You come on—"

The woman put out her hand, and in it was a wadded up bill and some change.

"I have money today. Not a lot, but enough for some tea." Stephen glanced at Joann when she sighed. "I promise it's all I want. A cup of hot tea. If you want, I'll take it to go, but I'd like to sit and get warm."

"Sit." Joann looked at him as she moved toward the pots of coffee and water and cups. "If Bob catches her in here again, he's going to go off. He don't like her much."

"Why?"

Joann shrugged at his question, and he looked back at the woman. She'd sat in the booth closest to the door and was spreading out her money. From where he was sitting, Stephen could see that she had one dollar and forty-seven cents. The cost of a cup of tea was a buck and a quarter. As Joann made her way to the girl, she picked up one of the dirty plates on the bar where Samuel had been eating and sat it on the table in front of the woman. He assumed it was to make it look as if she had ordered something if Bob came from the back.

"Thank you ever so much." She inhaled the steam coming off the cup as if she'd been smelling a fine wine. Stephen watched her as she eyed the sugar but didn't touch it. He'd bet anything that she was afraid she was pushing her limit and decided it wasn't worth the thought of getting tossed out over it. Stephen turned back to his own cup and reached out to the woman's mind.

It was locked. Not just blocked from him, but locked down. He couldn't even breach the thoughts that she was having now. Turning slightly, he looked at her and was startled to see her glaring at him. Stephen had never had anyone know he was in their mind before. Turning back, he looked at Joann, who was standing near the window looking at him.

"I don't know anything about her. Not even her name. She comes in about once a month to get something hot. Usually it's just tea or something." Her voice was low but he

10

could hear her just fine. "Once or twice she's come in to get warm and just sat quietly in her seat. Bob thinks she's a leech, but she's never done anything while in here."

"She's human?" Joann nodded and the bell rang again. Stephen didn't look this time, almost afraid to see who else would come in. When a sudden noise sounded behind him, he turned just in time to see the woman slicing the head off Jared's shoulders. He was gone in seconds.

Stephen was stunned. The long silver blade that skittered across the floor toward him was nothing compared to the one in the woman's hands. She didn't move as she looked at him and slid the sword into a scabbard that hung from her shoulder and down the front of her clothing. Closing up her coat, she looked as normal as she had when she'd entered.

"He was going to kill you and Joann." Stephen nodded but said nothing as his savior continued. "I don't know you, but Joann has been kind to me."

"So you would have let him kill me except for her?" Her shrug wasn't very encouraging. "I see. And for what reason do you suppose he wanted us dead?"

"Just you. She was a witness." The girl staggered slightly, and Stephen stood up. The sword was out again before he could take a step. "Move and I'll finish what he was going to do. I'd very much like it if you were to sit back down."

"I just wanted to see if you were all right." Her stance told him she wasn't going to allow him anywhere near her, and for some reason he was proud of her. "May I buy you breakfast for saving me?"

Bob came out of the back room then, and Stephen turned toward him. He was nearly ready to defend the woman when Joann started talking. She was telling him what had happened and that the stranger had kept murder and mayhem from ensuing. Looking back at the woman, Stephen wasn't really surprised to see that she was gone. Striding toward the door, he opened it to go after her, only to find himself in the arms of Samuel.

"She said you'd need me." Stephen asked him who. "Don't know. Some woman contacted me and said that the vamp was in trouble, that I was to get my ass here. Actually, she said to get my fucking ass here. She is a mite on the intense side if you ask me. But I did what she said. What's up?"

"Did she tell you who she was at all?" Samuel shook his head. "Jared came back with intent to kill me. I'm supposing because Joann was a witness to his crime, he was going to take her out as well. But whoever contacted you—and I'm only assuming it was my savior—pulled out a sword and killed him first."

"She saved your ass?" Stephen shook his head. "But here you stand. Wanna tell me why that is if she didn't save you?"

The humor in Samuel's voice pissed him off slightly, and he wanted to tell him to fuck off. It had been a strange morning, and he didn't think it was going to get any better with telling him that she'd only wanted to save Joann. He was just there when she did.

"I was secondary in her plan. And now because you have blocked my way, I don't know where to find her." He went to the booth and picked up the money. Taking it to his nose, he inhaled much like she had the cup and found nothing. Not a single scent was on the money, neither the bill nor the change. Nor was there anything on the full cup of tea. Stephen turned to Samuel. "I'll have to report this. The fucking bastard tried to kill me."

"Yeah. I hate when that happens." Stephen growled at his friend. "I'm only saying. But just so you know, the woman told me something else too. She said you're a target now. That I should keep you away from others until somebody finished the job they were sent out to do. She didn't sound all that upset that you might be killed soon."

"You mean there are others coming for me?" Stephen wasn't overly concerned about that. He'd been a hunted man for over three thousand years. "What for? I'm not doing anything to anyone."

"Don't know. But you being one of the others, as she called them, could get you killed. Other than you pissing in his oats this morning, what other reason could Jared have had to murder you?" Samuel sat in the chair he'd been in earlier and looked at the blade still laying where it had landed. "You recognize those markings?"

The handle as well as the blade was covered in scroll-like work. Stephen picked it up and looked at the small curls and swirls and realized it was writing. He put his hand around the pommel and looked at Samuel. This was bad. Really bad.

"It's my language. The language of my kind. This sword...I'm sure it's the original, and had been hanging in the castle where I grew up. It's from my family."

His crest, the one from his family, was on the tip of the pommel, and he stared at it as memory after memory flooded his mind. His father and mother, his little sister and brother...all of them dead now, and none of them anything but a distant memory after all this time. He started to tell Samuel what he felt like, needing to share for some reason, when he saw the spot of blood.

Walking toward it, he knew it had to be the woman's. The vampire Jared's blood would have disappeared when he did, leaving nothing behind to show that he'd ever been there. Kneeling down to it, he ran his fingers over the now cooled blood and brought it to his mouth. He licked it off his fingers before he could think of the several million reasons why he should not do it. The dizziness that swamped him made him fall to his ass, and it took him several seconds to realize that he'd passed out. Samuel smacking him in the face was his first clue. He grabbed his hand just as he drew back to hit him again.

"Christ. You scared the shit out of me. What the fuck happened?" Stephen stood up when Samuel helped him. "Stephen, what happened?"

He couldn't tell him. He doubted that Samuel would be upset. More than likely he'd think it funny. But if her blood gave him that sort of rush, then she could only be one thing to him, and he wasn't ready for a mate this late in his life. Never would suit him just fine and dandy. Instead of answering Samuel, he changed the subject.

"I'll have to contact the others to let them know what happened. And you'll need to help me with what the girl said to you about more gunning for me." Samuel looked like he was going to ask something but only nodded. "Jared was going to remove my head from my shoulders. I don't know about you, but that sort of pisses me off."

"I bet." Samuel walked to the clothes that were lying in a pile on the floor. Dust flittered about the room before it, like the man it had come from, disappeared as well. Stephen felt the pull of the sun take a little of his energy but ignored it for now. There were things he had to do before he could take his rest. Samuel looked at him with a cocked brow, and Stephen knew he'd missed something.

"You do know that whatever is going on, that girl might have more information than we do right now." Stephen nodded, knowing that he wasn't going to go looking for her no matter what. "I'll send some of the wolves that are wandering around the property over to your home. They can keep a look out and get some exercise too. They've been looking for things to get them running again."

Stephen pulled out his wallet and handed Bob what he had there. He knew that it was too much, that there was really very little damage done, but he wanted to get out, and haggling over the cost was just something he wasn't going to do. As he left the building, Samuel was right behind him.

"The girl? What did she say to you?" Stephen looked at Samuel when he didn't answer him. There was a knowing look on his face that Stephen didn't care for. "Whatever you're thinking, just get it out of your head right now."

"She's your mate." Stephen stopped walking and stared at his buddy. "I don't know how I know that other than your reaction to her blood, but I'm willing to bet that's what she is. Am I right?"

"No one likes a know-it-all." Samuel crossed his arms over his chest and did the eyebrow thing again. "Okay, yes, she's my mate, but I can't smell her, nor do I know a damned thing about her. And I'd very much like to keep it that way. And if you tell me it's a done deal, I may drain you."

Samuel's laughter did nothing to improve his mood. It wasn't so much the woman but all of it. He now had to go to the Vampire Council and explain to them how a slip of a woman had killed the leader of their little group. They were not going to be happy when he told them she'd gotten away too.

~~~

Clar moved to the cave slowly. She was hungry and pissed that she'd left her tea sitting there untouched. And she'd paid for it too. Moving deep into the cave, she sat down on the blanket she'd found this past summer and tried to brace herself for looking at her wound. The vamp she'd killed had hurt her when she'd knocked the sword from his hand. His claw-like hand had torn into her quicker than she'd expected.

He'd turned at the last second to grab at her arm, but had grazed her belly instead. Normally she would have been able to dodge him, but she'd been talking with the lion. Who knew that a lion would be in charge of so many different people? Taking a deep breath, she pulled up her shirt.

It was bleeding profusely, and when she tried to wipe away the blood, more moved across the seam of the wound like a zipper. When she finally got a look at it, she closed her eyes. He'd really hurt her.

"Figures. You do something for somebody and you get the shit knocked out of you." Standing up, she went to her medical kit. Over the years it had gotten larger because she cared for herself, and some of the things in it were things she'd picked up out of peoples' trash cans. Like the pain killers. But there were things in it she could use now, like the needle and thread, as well as the thick gauze and tape. It was going to be a long morning.

Debating on whether or not to take one of the pain pills now or later, she set it aside and pulled out the needle and thread. If she sewed it up, she might not get weaker. But knowing from past experience with supernaturals, their wounds didn't always act like the ones she got on her own. Starting a fire, she put a pot of water on the stones around it to heat up. The cave had a great many things in it that she'd made herself, and the fire pit was one of the things she loved the most. She looked around the cave and smiled. It was her home and she loved it.

The things she'd managed to bring here were great. Most of them were discards she'd picked up around the richer neighborhoods. But there was also the clothing bank that she'd hit in the warmer months when she had managed to get a coat, gloves, and a nice warm hat. The boots she'd found were not all that warm, but they did keep her feet dry. The blankets too had come from the clothing place. And then there were the crates.

She'd stacked them in such a way that they looked like a large wall unit. And she'd filled it with things that she'd found on her walks, along with her clothing and shoes. She also had some candles that people had used nearly up and tossed out. Some nights they were her only source of light.

It took her almost an hour to sew the wound together. The pain wasn't as bad as it could have been now that she'd taken the pills, but it still hurt like hell. Then there was the beating she'd taken before when some asshole had decided he wanted her to fuck him. When she lay back on her bed, she closed her eyes and tried to think of anything other than how badly she hurt. The vamp at the counter entered her thoughts.

He was handsome. No, that wasn't right. He was devastatingly handsome. His dark hair hung down past his shoulders, and his face looked like he might have been a model for some of the Greek gods she'd seen in the museums she used to go to. And when he'd stood up...Christ, he was so tall she knew that if she stood next to him she'd reach just to his chin, and she was tall at almost six foot.

"And he probably hits hard too." Clar smiled at the echo of her voice as it circled around and came back at her.

"Hello" would echo for twenty minutes it seemed sometimes, and Clar pulled her pillow from her head and put it on her wound so she could get a little more comfortable.

How had she gotten here? Smiling, she thought about her journey to her newest address. This had been the longest she'd been at one place since her flight away from her family all those years ago. In the eleven years, she'd moved about eight times and this one, this last one had been over eight months. But the weather was turning now, so she'd have to find something with more heat if she wanted to live through another winter. Her mother…it took her breath away when she thought of her and her death. Her mother would have a fit if she could see her little girl now.

Clarice Kelley had left home at the age of seventeen. Her only thought at that time was to get as much distance between her and her stepfather as she could. If there was ever a meaner man in the world, she never wanted to meet him. Her stepfather, Edward Barron, was a prick of the first order. And he hated her with all his being.

"I suppose it didn't help that I didn't care overly much for him either." And she hadn't. She wasn't really his daughter, not even his stepdaughter, but a "product," as he'd called her, of an unfortunate first marriage her mom had had. Clar's real dad had died a few months before she was born, but she knew a great deal about him. Clinton Kelley had been a bad choice in marriage, as her stepfather had said. But he'd loved her mother more than anything, and he'd died proving it to her.

Edward, as she'd taken to calling him since her mother married him, had made no bones about how much he hated her. He wanted a son…many sons, he told her once, but she would be his pawn. A pawn in what she'd had no idea at the time, but he'd told her later…the day she left, as a matter of fact. And just a mere month after she'd gotten out of the hospital following injuries she'd suffered when her mom was killed. Had it only been three months after her mother died that her stepfather had tried to make her do something her mother would have killed him over?

"I've made some arrangements now that your mother is not here to tell me no. You'll marry my vice-president, and he'll take you out of my sight." She'd shaken her head, and he slapped her hard enough to knock her off the chair she'd been told to sit in. "I didn't ask you if you wanted to, Kelley, but said you would. The marriage will take place right after Christmas, and you'll be gone from this house for good. The only time I ever want to see your face again is when there is no other choice. It's cost me a great deal to have this fixed, and you'll be a dutiful wife and give him whatever he wants."

"I don't care how much it cost you. I'm not marrying an old bastard on your say-so." She moved before he could hit her this time, and he lunged for her. Clar had kicked out and got him in the balls and smiled when he cried out. "Next time you think to order me around, Edward, I suggest you do it with me tied up."

"You're going to pay for that." She kicked him again, this time in the head. With a quick check of his pulse when he didn't get up right away, she knew that she couldn't be so lucky. It was too much to hope that he was dead. And with another kick to his big gut, she walked out and up to her room to gather what she could. Once she was outside, Clar had never looked back.

"But he still tries to bring me in." Just a year ago she'd had to move on again. This time she'd moved almost within spitting distance to her old home, and chuckled every time she walked past one of his minions. None of them would recognize her now. She was a good hundred pounds lighter than she'd been at seventeen, and her blonde hair had darkened over the years. Sometimes Clar didn't even know herself when she chanced a look in a mirror.

Closing her eyes, she tried to let the pain pills she'd taken do their magic. Thoughts of the vampire kept her awake more than she thought necessary, and when someone touched her mind, she nearly kept them out. But the lion was trying to reach her, and she let him in just enough to see what he wanted.

You should know that the council needs to speak to you. Ignoring him for the moment, she waited for him to continue. *I don't suppose you'd tell me how badly you're hurt, would you? I'm concerned only because a vampire hurt you, and Stephen is upset.*

Who's that? She hadn't meant to say anything, but she found she wanted to know if this Stephen person knew the man she'd killed.

He is the vampire you saved. Clar liked the name but said nothing to the lion. *My name is Samuel, Samuel Payne. If you need anything, you can —*

No thanks. I've got everything I need where I am. What else do you want? And don't give me any bullshit about how you were concerned about my welfare. I'm not stupid.

I am concerned about you. Stephen is as well. He's resting now but wanted me to see if I could see if you'd meet with him. A lie. She had no idea why she knew it but did and called him on it. *Okay, he'd just as soon never meet you, but I don't think that's going to work either. He's tasted your blood.*

Clar sat up quickly, tearing at the wound. He'd tasted her blood? That wasn't possible. They'd never touched, much less been close enough for him to bite her. Then she looked down at her bloodstained pants and knew that had to be it. Some of her blood had been left behind.

"Why would he taste my blood?" She'd spoken out loud, her voice echoing around her. But the man answered her as well. Clar felt her body turn to ice.

He wanted to know who saved his life. You should also know that you're his mate. Do you know what that is? She did, but didn't answer the lion. She had to get things going and find a safe place, if there was one, to hide out until she was strong enough to fight him if need be.

Clar knew that in her current condition, leaving was out of the question, so she had to make do with what she had. Looking around the cave, she wondered if she could go deeper, but decided that if she locked herself up tight, he'd never find her.

You tell him to mind his own business and you do the same. I'm fine. If you contact me again, you're going to hurt like a motherfucker, so I would advise against it. He told her he couldn't do that. She was in his pride now. *Fuck your pride. I'm not going to tell you this again. Stay the fuck away from me and you'll be just fine.*

Locking down her head, she felt him try to get to her again. The pain she sent to him was a bit too much, she knew, but if he got the message right away, maybe he'd stop. But for some reason she doubted he'd be that smart. The vampire either. Pulling her blanket over her chilled body, she lay there trying to think what to do now. This was all she needed, a pain in the ass lion and a vampire that thought she'd be his next meal.

Chapter 2

Vinnie watched Stephen as he paced the large office. The faeries that had been there when he'd entered were now on the ceiling, and probably would stay there until Stephen left. It wasn't as if they were afraid of him biting them, but he just might step on one of them. Vinnie looked at his computer when it chimed.

The email had been one he'd been waiting on. And since Stephen had not said a single word other than he needed to talk since he'd entered, Vinnie decided to work. He leaned forward in his chair to answer the mail. He was nearly finished with it when Stephen finally sat back down.

"Are you going to ignore me when I come to talk to you?" Vinnie finished the letter before he hit send. When he was finished, he looked at his friend.

"First of all, you should know that you are in a pissy mood, and while I think it's funny, I won't put up with you taking it out on me. Secondly, you've been here for over an hour pacing this office like it was your job and have not said a fucking thing. I have, believe it or not, a job that requires me to keep abreast of things going on around me. Unlike you, I enjoy working." When Stephen started to speak, Vinnie cut him off. "If this has anything to do with the woman who saved your life, I agree with you. Stay the fuck away from her and you'll be just fine."

"I don't think I can do that anymore. And I'm assuming you heard this information from Big Mouthed Samuel." Vinnie shook his head. "Then who? You didn't get it from Joann down at the diner, did you?"

"Nope. Kennedy told me." Vinnie laughed when Stephen cursed. Kennedy had only said it in passing and he'd gotten most of the information from Samuel. But it was fun to see Stephen get all worked up about it. "She said you should find the girl, fuck her until she can't walk, and have a passel of kids."

She'd not said that, but again he was having entirely too much fun not to rib his friend as much as he could. He'd wait to tell him he had someone go to the diner who had "talked" to the seat and cup where the girl had been, but wasn't sure that was a good idea either. Vinnie knew a great deal about the faceless woman now, thanks to his new partner, Hawk. The man was a miracle worker when it came to knowing about such things.

It took Stephen another ten minutes before he sat back down. Vinnie had answered two more emails and had contracted a job that he'd been wanting to do for years now. When it looked like his friend was calmer, he turned off the monitor and leaned back again.

"She's hurt. Not just from the vampire, but she's got a couple of broken ribs. Hawk isn't sure what happened there, but she is hurting." Grateful that Stephen didn't ask him how Hawk knew, Vinnie continued. "She's running from a man, but his name is vague or she's doing a fucking fantastic job of keeping it locked in that mind of hers. And she's living nearby. A cave, he thinks."

"Samuel said she hurt him when he tried to contact her, blasted back at his head like a cannon going off. He seems to think that she's a clairvoyant or something. The fact that she knew the man trying to kill me was a vampire as well as Samuel being a lion leads me to believe that she's had some contact with our kind." Vinnie nodded. He'd thought the same thing when Samuel had told him that she'd called him lion, not by his name.

"Her name is Clar, but I don't think that's really it. And so you know, the faeries are out looking for her. I figured they'd have a better chance than wolves or anything else in finding where she had hidden." Stephen nodded, and Vinnie continued. "I've gone out too, but all I could find was a few humans hanging around where they shouldn't be and I ran them off. I think…she's being chased, but I don't know by who."

Stephen sat there for a long time, and Vinnie knew he was thinking how to ask him. He wouldn't tell him anything unless Hawk okayed it. The man was terrified that someone would find out that he could talk to things that didn't have a pulse. But when Stephen got up to pace again, Vinnie continued telling him what they knew.

"Her abilities aside, did you get anything else from her blood other than that she's your mate? Like what she might be?" Stephen shook his head and stared out the darkened window of Vinnie's office. Several of the faeries came down from the ceiling to sit on his desk. One of them, Yve, sat on his keyboard and looked up at him.

"She's been found. She is not…she will need him, but if he does not want her, I will have them leave her where she is." Meaning, Vinnie knew, that she'd let her die. "It is better that she die than to be unwanted by him, my lord. We can

25

only do so much with someone like her. And her mother was someone we all know of."

"It's not our decision to make. And you'll tell me later what you know of her mother. Deal?" Yve nodded, and Stephen turned to look at him when he spoke. "They've found her. And she might not be in the best of shape. Yve will leave her there if you'd really like to be rid of her."

"She's dying." Vinnie nodded, and Stephen sat down. "I...can they take me to her? Will they? I don't know what I'll do when I find her, but can they take me to her?"

"I will not, my lord." Yve stood up and flew to Stephen. "We will not have her suffer at the hands of another. She is kind, it is said, and when she leaves an area, she makes it better than when she was there. Her footprint is very small when she is in residence to one of our places."

"You know that she's my mate, don't you?" Yve nodded but said nothing as Stephen continued. "I don't want a mate this late in my life. I'm thousands of years old, and she will... I don't know what to do with her."

"Love her comes to mind." Yve didn't say anything when Stephen shook his head. But she did come back to Vinnie and looked up at him. She would tell him if he ordered her to, but he really didn't want to do that. As a dragon, the faerie cared for him in ways that no one else could.

He asked Yve how bad it was. "She will be gone by morning if nothing is done. Her fever is taking its toll on her, as is the loss of blood. I fear that she will be a great loss if no one cares for her. What will you do if he chooses to leave her there?"

He would do nothing, and she knew it. It was not his place to care for another man's mate. But he also knew that if Stephen did let her die, he would no longer be his friend.

There were some things that could not be forgiven. And leaving a female to die, of any species, was something that should never be done

"Tell me where she is. I'll care for her." They both looked at Stephen, who looked as if the weight of the world was on his shoulders. "I don't have to mate with her now that I've taken her blood, but I don't want her to die alone either."

Yve moved back to Stephen and touched his head before she spoke. "You will do as you promise to me, Master Vampire, or I will rain a hell on you that will be a match to nothing you've ever seen before."

"I promise you I will care for her. I won't love her or keep her as my mate, but I will make sure that she has what she needs to live."

For some reason, Vinnie didn't think it would be that simple. And he had a feeling Yve didn't think so either.

They all left together, and Vinnie contacted Samuel to let him know what they were doing. Samuel said he'd meet them in the glen below the mountain where she was, and Kennedy said she'd bring one of the doctors from the clinic. Yve rode on his shoulder as he shifted and took her there. Vinnie looked into the cave, as he was the first to arrive.

The place smelled of death. But the room where she lay was in direct contrast to what he'd been led to believe a homeless person might have lived like. Everything was in neat order, from her firewood stacked nearby, the flames now gone cold, to the walls where she'd put books and candles on the small outcrops. He even liked the way she'd used old crates with vines woven in them to keep them straight. Vinnie walked toward the bundle on the floor as far from the opening as possible without going too deep into the cave.

She was still breathing, and the heat coming from her made him think of the fire that burned in his belly most of the time. Her hair was soaking wet and tangled about her head. There were scratches on her face and a bruise just below her left eye. Vinnie wondered if she'd done that when she'd saved Stephen. He pulled the blankets from her body just as someone appeared in the doorway.

Stephen looked…well, he was going to say pale, but he always looked that way. But the man did look afraid. Of what, he wasn't sure, but he knew that some of it had to do with being in the dark place. Stephen had hated closed, dark places for as long as he'd known him. Vinnie looked at Samuel when his big cat came into the room just behind Stephen.

"She is still with us." Yve turned to look at him before she continued speaking. "She will not last the night if help is not given to her soon."

"I told you I'd help her, and I will." Stephen came forward and stopped just short of her body. "She's burning up. Why is she so hot and shaking?"

"She is human. The fever is taking her and will soon finish what the wound has not. The wound is infected and will need to be cleaned. I can do that if you wish." Stephen shook his head at Yve and knelt down beside the woman. He touched his finger to her cheek and his face seemed to harden.

"She wasn't hurt like this yesterday. Or if she was, it hadn't marred her skin yet. Who dared touch her?" No one answered him as he opened his wrist. "When she is fed, do you think she will need more care than that?"

"You plan on leaving her here?" Vinnie was glad that Samuel had asked, because he was sure that he would have hit him first before asking. "Christ man, even if you do bring her back from death, staying here won't do her a lick of good."

"I'm not leaving her. And thank you ever so much for thinking I'm that much of a cold bastard. I meant before I could move her from here, not leave her." Stephen pressed his wrist to her mouth, and all of them watched as blood trailed down her mouth to her chin. "She's not taking it in. What do I do?"

"Tell her to drink. You can touch her mind now, I'm betting. With her out, she can't hide from you." Vinnie sat down across from Stephen and pinched the woman's nose. "Tell her to drink. She will have to do something with not being able to breathe this way."

Stephen commanded her to drink, but it didn't really do much good. Her heart rate slowed even more until Vinnie was sure she was simply going to die to spite them all. When Yve landed on her forehead and then moved toward her ears, Vinnie was sure she was going to use her magic. But all she did was move her hair from her temple and show the scar to them all.

"This is how she can use her mind like she does. I've heard that she was wounded when her mother passed. I do not know if it is true or not, but she has a great gift now that she did not have before." Vinnie looked at Stephen when he ran his finger over the large scar. "You would do well to remember her upbringing, Master Silva. The lady has been through more than you in all your lifetimes. And has lost a great deal that she cannot ever forgive."

When a small moan came from the woman who had lain so still, all of them watched as she swallowed twice before she moaned again. When her hand came out and curled around Stephen's wrist, Vinnie got up to leave. They were going to be a couple even against Stephen's wishes.

~~~

Stephen had brought her to his home by his own magic, and was glad now that he'd taken care to make sure that his house was always ready for guests...guests of any kind. He'd even had some of his subjects go back to her cave and gather what they could find and bring it back as well. There was no way she was going back there, even if she didn't stay with him. When she was settled in one of the upper bedrooms, he went to the kitchen to talk to his butler, Kasen.

"I don't know what she will eat or when she'll wake up, but could you please make sure there is something here for her when and if she wants it?" He nodded and Stephen had the uncontrollable urge to explain more. "I don't want her here, and she won't be staying once she is on the mend. But while here I'd like for her to get the best care. If you could make sure that she has everything she needs, then we can make sure she gets out of here quicker."

"Of course, my lord." Kasen looked up the staircase and back at him before continuing. "The faeries have sent over a few of their kind to watch over her as well. Will I be...I will need to...sire, I'm not sure what to feed them."

"I think they'll take care of that part." He really didn't know, but a faerie had come back with him when he'd brought Clar to his home. Leith was now a part of his home, or at least until Clar left. She would be her protector from now on. He told Kasen about the little person.

"Will she...sire, I'm not sure what you want me to do with her. And the others. There are so many of them in the room with the young woman." And there were too. Hundreds of them had come to see her and they were coming and going. So much that he'd left a window open in the bathroom for them to come and go as they pleased, sliding under the door to enter or leave the bedroom.

"Just leave them alone and they'll leave us alone. Once the girl is healed enough to leave, they'll be gone." Stephen started out of the room and turned back. "Kasen, what do you know of telepathy?"

"Nothing much, sire. Shall I see what I can find out? Is the young woman…does she have this ability?" Stephen nodded. "I see. I will see what I can find for you and have it when you rise. Will you require anything else?"

"No. I guess that's it." He started for the lower levels and turned instead to the stairs leading to where she was resting. He would check on her again before going down, he told himself. When he entered the room, several of the faeries flew to the ceiling, and he wanted to tell them to get out. But all he did was sit in the chair and look at Clar. One of the braver little ones landed on his knee.

"We're afraid of you, sire." Stephen nodded. He was a vampire, after all, and faerie blood was like a drug to him. They were right to be afraid. "It is said that you have been cured of the need of us. Is that true?"

"Yes. Ana, the one that works with Kaleb, took that away for me. She said so long as I was in one of the households of the other members of Samuel's pride, I'd not have a need to drink from you. Before we arrived, I had Kaleb come and put the same spell on this house temporarily. When the woman here leaves, my house will return to a faerie-free home." The little man nodded, then stepped up to the bed. "You guys, you know her then?"

"Most of us do. Her mother we know a good deal better. There was a garden that she cared for not far from here. It has not been the same since the mother has gone from there, but we do the best we can. The man who lives in the house alone, he would destroy it if he could, but he cannot because of the fact that she put it in the will that way. She told us that it would be that way forever."

Stephen knew that forever to a human was not the same as it would be to an immortal such as he was, and he thought the faerie was. When Stephen touched Clar's hand, he could feel the chill of it and covered it with the heated blanket that he'd had put on the bed for her.

"You know her name then?" The little faerie didn't answer, and Stephen looked at him. "I don't think I know yours either, as a matter of fact."

"I'm Daldon. My daughter, Ana, works for Sir Kaleb. My missus, she is the one who will watch over this young girl when she is better." He looked up at him and frowned. "You do not wish to keep her as your mate even though she is yours? Surely that cannot be true."

"It is and no, I don't. I don't want a mate, nor do I know what to do with one. When she's better, I'll make sure she has all she needs to be safe, but I won't keep her here." Stephen didn't like the way Daldon looked at him and changed the subject. "There is a man in the kitchen of this house; his name is Kasen. He works for me and he knows that if you or she needs anything, you're to tell him and he'll make sure you have it. I'll be resting during the day. And then I have to go to the council and explain something to them."

"The one that my lady killed." Stephen nodded. "He would have ended your life that day had she not taken the time to help you. It is so like her to do something like that. The other day when those men tried to take her body, she told everyone to leave so that we'd not get hurt. But they did not listen to her."

"Someone tried to rape her?" Daldon nodded and sat down on Clar's belly. The wound was there, but he was so small that Stephen knew that she wasn't feeling it, but it bothered him nonetheless.

"They did. I think they hit her a great deal. I was not there, mind you, but heard about it. Several of the pixies were with her when it happened." Daldon got up to move closer to her face and stared down at her as he continued. "There is none sweeter than this one, but no one is meaner when she needs to be."

Stephen had a feeling he was right. He'd not seen either side of her as yet, but he'd bet everything he owned that she'd be a bitch when needed. Getting up, he moved to the door; his body was shutting down. Looking back at the little man, he tried to tell him what he felt.

"She's my mate. You understand that, correct?" Daldon smiled and nodded. "I'm not going to claim her. I have given her my blood so I will always have a connection to her, but I can't have her in my life. It's not...I'm much too old and set in my ways to change now. Neither of us will be happy if she tries to change me."

"You think it will be that easy, my lord?" Stephen didn't answer, but apparently he wasn't required to. "Things have a way of working out for the best. You say you are old and set in your ways, and that she will change you, correct? Perhaps she will simply like you for who you are."

"I don't even like me for what I am." With that he turned and left the room. There were things he had to get finished before he could rest, and one of them was to make sure his house was secure. He had no idea who was chasing Clar, if that was even her name, but he would make sure she was safe while in his house. And he had to find out who the men were that had tried to rape her. An hour later, Stephen was dragging himself to the lower levels to rest.

A sound woke him, and he laid there for several seconds before he opened his eyes. The room was still in semi-darkness, and the light that always burned was still on. But he could feel someone there...or maybe, something. Sitting up, he let a little of his beast go and spoke.

"Whoever you are, it's not just dangerous that you're in my room uninvited, but it could be deadly as all hell for you to be. Show yourself." No one answered, but he heard the flare of a match just before a bright light showed a person's face.

"You should know that finding you was harder than I thought it would be." Stephen didn't move when the woman blew out the match and the room darkened again. Using some of his considerable magic, he lit the room so that there were no shadows anywhere.

"Who are you, and what the hell do you want?" *She wasn't there*, was his first thought. Just a projection of herself, which meant that they had at one time exchanged blood. Otherwise, she'd never had been able to come to him.

"I'm Velvet. Velvet December. It's not my real name, of course. Don't you just love that name? Back when you and I were lovers, it was just plain old Sally Shunt." He still had no idea, but rose from his bed and reached for his robe. He was in the habit of sleeping in the nude, and felt uncomfortable with her in the room with him in such a state of undress. Her laughter made his skin crawl, and it triggered the necessary memory to tell him who she was.

"You're supposed to be dead. I made sure that you were brought before the committee back then, and they told me you were put to death." She shrugged. "Well? Why are you here and not dust on someone's shoes?"

"I was sentenced, but not to death. I suppose they thought I'd eventually get dug up and the sun would take me, but that patch of earth was never good for anything once they put me there." She moved about his room, looking at things but unable to touch them. "You did me a great injustice by turning me in, Stephen. I'm very upset with you. I'd like to know what you plan to do about making it up to me."

"I don't give a shit what you are. And as far as making anything up to you? You can fuck off for all I care. I want you to get out of here and leave me to my life." Her laughter again. It grated on his nerves like nails down a chalkboard. "Say what you want, then leave. Whatever you think you have to say to me is going to fall on deaf ears. I could care less about you."

"You did at one time." He had too, he remembered, until she'd betrayed him and he'd cut her out of his life. And he remembered how extremely easy it had been too. But she spoke again before he could let that sour memory form. "You were going to live your days with me. You said you'd care for me and make sure that no harm came to me. Is turning me over to the Vampire Committee how you keep your promises?"

The Vampire Committee had been a long time ago, back when, as vampires, they were more in the shadows and darkness than they were now. Now, he was a productive part of society; back then he was simply a monster. Now the council was more forward thinking, a more human friendly group that not only consisted of vampires but a few other species as well. Before—a long time before—they had thought to change the bad and make them a better vampire. Stephen still didn't agree with most of what they did these days, but he did like their way of thinking on some things.

"And what of yours, Velvet? Did you ever think how your antics would fall to me? How your killing sprees would look to the council?" He snorted and sat down. "You told them that I was a part of your group, the leader of you all so that you'd only get a slap on the wrists while I was beheaded. What of your love then?"

"You were such a pussy back then. And I'm betting that you're no different now than you were back then. A fucking pussy that always keeps to the rules so that you're the all mighty Stephen when it comes to vampires." Her anger blasted through her; what she would consider her carefully laid out plan to get him to come back to her was quickly falling apart. "You never did play. What the fuck are you doing now? Playing the concerned and wealthy human? How lazy you've become."

"Lazy?" Stephen pretended to consider her words. "I suppose you could call me that. I work hard to make myself blend in, something you never wanted to do. And as for my wealth? Yes, I do have a great deal of it. More than I could ever spend. But I like that too. I give much more than most humans make in their entire lifetime to causes that mean something to me. So I suppose you could call me lazy. But I'd call me...happy."

"Happy? Happy?" She was shrieking now, and he didn't even try to hide his smile. "What the fuck do you have to be happy about? You don't do anything, not as a vampire. Why aren't you out there showing the fucking humans what we are? Kill some of them. Christ, you're not even drinking from them, are you?"

"I do. When it suits me." Wherever she was, he knew that things were being destroyed. He could see her lifting things and throwing them, but not exactly what they were. Back when they'd been together, her anger had scared him a little. Not for him, but what she'd do to the ones around them when she unleased it. Nothing, nor anyone, was safe from her wrath.

When she seemed to calm, he looked around his lair. There was nothing here to give her any clue as to where he might be other than a dark room. And he was reasonably sure that she hadn't found him physically either. But she would. Stephen had kept his name over the centuries simply because he'd move rather than change his name. It was simpler.

"I came to see if you and I could take up where we left off, but I can see that's never going to happen. Even if you did want me back, I'd—"

"I don't want you." She growled, and he smiled. "And I want you to stop looking for me as well. We're through. And as soon as I'm finished talking to you, I'm contacting the council to let them know that you've been released." Velvet moved toward him, but he simply let her. She couldn't touch him, and even if she could, he was a good deal stronger than her on her best day. "You'll heed what I say. If you do not, your maker will hear about it."

"You mean the one I killed this evening?" She tossed back her head and laughed. "After today I will make it my life's work to find you and destroy you. Everything you love, everything you care about, I will kill and tear apart. You'll regret what you've done to me. And if the council thinks they can control me, or even catch me, they'll die as well. I'm coming for you, Stephen. And when I find you, you're going to pay."

Her image disappeared, and Stephen sat there for several minutes trying to block his mind from her. It was difficult, but he did manage to get most of her attempts stopped. There would always be a slight connection, but he hoped that it would be too small for her to find him. Of course, it would be equally difficult to find her, but right now he had too many people depending on him to let her near them. Going out of his lair, he headed toward the stairs. The woman had to be cared for first and foremost.

Chapter 3

Samuel wasn't sure what he was supposed to do while hanging around the house watching the woman in Stephen's house, but here he was. Stephen had called him first thing this evening when he'd risen and asked him to come here. Stephen had a meeting and said he'd explain things when he got finished. That had been over two hours ago. And in all that time, the woman had never moved.

She was pretty, he supposed. Pale, but not too bad, and her hair was dark. He could see now that someone had washed it. The clothes she had on now, he knew, belonged to Stephen, because there was no way they belonged to her. They were entirely too large for her frame, not to mention he doubted she'd be wearing a silk dress shirt.

"She is a wonder, is she not?" Samuel looked over at the faerie and nodded. "I know that you will not believe this, but she is very special to us. Some of us have watched over her since she was born. Her mother, Cleo, would bring her to the fields when she came to think. I believe it was to hide from the human whom she had wed, but I did not know either of them then. It is a great honor to watch one such as her."

"Is she human?" Leith shook her head and flew to sit on his knee. He never really felt comfortable when they did that, but said nothing to her. Samuel was always terrified of squashing one of them. He looked at the woman again. "Do you think her stepfather is the one that she's hiding from?"

"I believe he is. He is not a nice person and is the cause of her wound. And though it is a good thing, she was in a great deal of pain when it came to pass. When her mother passed from this world, he was very angry with this child. Cleo had been gone too long and had not been there when he returned from his place of work. He found her in the hospital with the daughter, and he…we all know that he murdered her. The man claimed he had no idea that her car would be robbed. He has been free because humans are afeard of him." Leith moved to the bed and sat near the woman's face. "Her name is Clarice Kelley. I found it today. Her mother never told us her name because we were afraid of knowing it. Do you know why?"

"A name holds power." She nodded and smiled at him. "Her stepfather? Do you happen to know his name? Stephen will need to know it so that he can make sure she is safe."

"He will not care. He does not want her. It is very sad when a man does not want what does belong to him." Samuel knew this, and it bothered him that Stephen was so set in his ways that he'd not even give them a chance to make it work. "When she leaves here, I will follow her. There will be several of us to try and keep her safe."

"And how do you propose to do that?" He flushed when he realized what he'd said. "I'm sorry. I just don't understand how someone as small as you can do much for a human. Or anyone for that matter. It's not that I don't believe you'll try, but I just don't see how it would help her if she's in trouble." He remembered when a group of them had killed a person once. Had simply torn him apart without even enough to know that he'd been there.

"We have our own magic, Master Samuel. And when we take on the job of watching someone, more is granted to us. I have my magic, plus what was given to me when I asked and was granted the job of keeping her safe. I can take on a man your size and then some." Samuel started to ask her to show him, but Leith suddenly stood up and stared hard at Clar. "She is dreaming of him. Of Master Stephen. Her heart is pounding. Mayhap he is in trouble because of what she did."

Samuel could hear her heart beating. Leith was right, it had started beating a good deal faster. Thinking of his friend, he touched Stephen's mind just before Clar moved on the bed.

I'm fine. Pissed, but fine. I was going to tell you when I got back, but there is a vampire out looking for me. She has no idea where I am, but apparently neither does the council know where she is. The fucking whore. They were under the impression she was still buried...the woman, not the council. Though there are days I'd gladly bury them. Samuel didn't have a clue what he meant, but Stephen explained at least a little of what he was talking about. *She had been sentenced to death, this other vampire. Back in the day, we were a lot more tolerant of our kind, and she was buried in a silver-encased casket with spells put on it. She was to be there forever, but someone found her.*

Found her or happened upon the casket? Samuel regretted his question after a few minutes. Stephen didn't answer him for so long he got up to go to the window. He'd be a little more diligent from now on. Especially with his own family.

You'd think that would be their first question, wouldn't you? But no, they're trying to figure out where the silver has gone. They seemed to be concerned that someone robbed them. Fucking morons. So I'm still trying to figure that one out. According to the humans that live around where she was buried, they'd been hearing all sorts of things at night until they finally called the police. Once they got involved, someone had the bright idea to call in a dozer, and they disturbed her grounds. Samuel looked at Leith when she came to fly around him. He put out his hand so she'd have somewhere to light as Stephen continued. *They released her, and she went on a feeding frenzy. There are nineteen dead bodies here that should never have been. Four of them are children.*

I'm sorry. Samuel looked out the window again and could see the wolves that watched the grounds. He wasn't sure, but he thought there were several more than there had been last week when he'd been here. *You've beefed up security because you're afraid she'll come here to get to Clar. Oh, by the way, her name is Clarice Kelley. Leith just told me.*

Thanks. I'll talk to her when I get there. The council is trying to figure out where the vampire has gone. I'm thinking anywhere but where we are currently, but they have rules. Samuel laughed when Stephen growled low. *And they think that I should take the place of Jared. In no uncertain terms, I've told them no.*

And how is that working for you? Another growl, and Samuel knew that it wasn't working at all. *What about your realm? Will they expect you to do both?*

Yes. There was a long pause, and while he was waiting on Stephen to say more, Samuel explained to Leith what was going on. She flew back to Clar and sat on her chest again. They, too, he knew, would beef up their own security around Clar. When Stephen spoke this time, there was a good deal of anger spilling between their connections. *I'm coming home. Can you please do me a favor and ask your wolves to patrol the grounds more? I have a connection with their boss, of course, but right now I'm not so sure I'd be all that nice, and I think I've already pissed off enough people.*

"Sire, she is waking a little." Samuel looked over at the bed when Leith spoke and stared into the most amazing eyes he'd ever seen. The woman was indeed awake. She never said anything, but she looked at him for several long moments before she closed her eyes again.

Stephen, she just woke for a minute or two. And good Christ, you should have seen her eyes. I think…Christ, it was like looking into an ocean, they're so blue. Stephen said something, but Samuel didn't hear him. He was still trying to wrap his mind around the fact that saying her eyes were blue was like calling him different. They were like both the heavens and oceans with a mix of everything warm and fuzzy. A few minutes later, Stephen walked into the room.

~~~

"What do you mean you've no idea where she is? I asked you to find her, and you come in here with excuses. I need her found now. It's been years since I started this search; don't you have any idea where she is?" Edward didn't really need her, but it was the principle of the matter. He owned her ass, and as far as he was concerned, she owed him. And until the debt was paid, he'd look for her.

He was well off…very well off as a matter of fact. His poor dearly departed wife had left him in good shape. Cleo Kelley-Barron had made sure that there was enough money for her daughter if she passed, and that had doubled when she'd been murdered in a carjacking all those years ago. It couldn't have gone better if he'd planned it. Which he sort of did.

He'd only meant to have her scared. The fucking woman would not take the limo that was ready when she was for all pain in the world. Cleo would drive herself around with that brat of a daughter as if she were nothing more than a poor homeless person. And that car was an

43

embarrassment to him. To say it was old was a gross understatement. It was older than her daughter had been.

"It's mine and it's paid for. Why do you care about what it looks like? It's not like you ride anywhere with me." And he never would so long as she was with the product. "I love my freedom to come and go as I please. Perhaps if you drove yourself once in a while, you'd be surprised at how much money you could save."

That had been another sore spot about her. She never took the money all that seriously. He'd have to make her buy a dress for any function they were asked to attend. Cleo would have worn the same dress over and over had he not stepped in and had a dress sent to her. Finally, he'd had to toss out her old dresses and have new ones sent to her. That had become harder and harder as the years went on as well. To be honest—and Edward was nearly always honest with himself concerning his wife and the product—he was nearly at the end of her being his wife anyway.

"We have all sorts of feelers out looking for her. Maybe she's dead and nobody knew who she was." Edward only shook his head at his latest hump-boy, Tony Webster. It was what he called all the flunkies that worked for him. They'd either hump their asses or he'd find someone that would. And this guy was proving to be very good as his job.

"I have a man at the FBI that knows to look for someone with her prints." Edward leaned back in his chair and thought of the fat blob that he'd gotten as part of the deal with Cleo.

"Do you suppose she's moved to another country? I mean it's possible, I suppose. And even if she only went down south, it would still be difficult to find her." Tony sat down in the chair across from his desk as he continued trying to find information. He supposed he would ask. He'd been on this assignment for only about three months when his predecessor had suddenly disappeared.

"She hasn't applied for a passport, and even if she changed her name, she'd need money to do that. From what I've learned, she didn't take anything with her, and what little money she might have had is long gone by now." Which was true. When she'd kicked him that day and ran out of the house, the staff had found her little stash of money. There had been several thousand dollars in it, and that had pissed him off as well. But she was resourceful and always had been, so he knew if she wanted something, even if it was to hide from him, she'd be able to make it happen.

"Sir, do you think she might have changed her appearance?" Edward looked at Tony, trying to think what he might be talking about. He was worried about that, his inability to stay focused. A doctor's appointment was set for next week. He wanted a full check-up as well as a training session set up to help him with the little pot belly he'd acquired over the Thanksgiving holiday.

"You mean cut her hair? I would say that's it. If you're talking about her weight, I highly doubt it. She ate like she was never going to get another meal and packed it in just in case." Edward shivered at the thought of her eating habits. "I think once a fat ass, always one. No, she's still obese. And maybe bigger if anything."

"Is there a possibly that she might have gotten someone to give her a new identity? Maybe a new name where she could be working?" Edward doubted that as well. She was simply too lazy. Resourceful, yes, in a way that she'd get others to do things for her rather than do them herself, but not all that smart.

"I think she's at some fat farm hiding out from me just to piss me off. Someone as lazy as she'd been as a kid will have taken that over into their adult life."

Which sadly wasn't true of the girl. She'd been fat, yes...really fat compared to her tiny mother, but she'd not been lazy. He'd seen her working in the gardens and fields of flowers her mother had planted for hours on end, digging up roots and planting them somewhere else. He'd have burned the entire gardens to the ground but for the people in their town. They had memorialized the place in her honor, and he was sure they'd turn on him if he did it. Fucking bitch had made it so he couldn't do what he'd wanted there, and he hated her all the more for it. Of course, the will was what really stopped him and had him spending money on keeping the stupid garden up. It was minimal at best, but he was doing as he'd been told or the money would dry up.

"Sir?" Edward turned to look again and was startled by the phone ringing. Picking it up, he started to say his name when he was cut off. There was too much background noise for him to understand the person and asked them to repeat themselves.

"I said, are you Edward Barron? Christ, are all humans as stupid as you are?" Edward had no idea what the woman was talking about but didn't get a chance to ask her. "Are you working with a man by the name of Stephen Silva?"

"Stephen? Yes. We have a good working relationship and have worked together for a good many years." Edward had a sudden thought that Stephen was leaving his firm for another. He hoped to Christ not. Ninety-percent of the advertising company he owned was working because of his payments each month. "Who did you say this was?"

"I didn't. And I won't either until I know you better."
Her voice purred across the line and Edward felt his dick
harden. "Do you want to get to know me better, Eddie boy?
Would you like for me to suck your cock and have you come
down my throat?"

His body reacted as if she were doing just what she'd
said. His cock was so hard that he was dizzy from it. When
he glanced up, he could see Tony staring at him as if he
knew what was going on beneath the desk. Edward waved
him out of the room and leaned back to give some relief to
his cock before talking to the woman.

"I don't know who you are, but I don't care for that sort
of talk from someone I don't know." He stroked his cock as
he continued. "What do you think you're going to
accomplish by speaking to me that way?"

"Making you come? Would you like that?" The purr
again made Edward close his eyes as he unbuckled his
pants. There was no way he was going to come like this,
from a phone call, but he was aching to be freed, and he did
so. As soon as his cock was straining from the opening of his
pants, Edward wrapped his hand around it and fisted
himself.

"Are you giving yourself a hand job? Are you thinking
of my mouth sucking you down?" He was but said nothing
to her. He knew she could hear his breathing and it didn't
bother him as much as he was sure it should. "I'm going to
do that to you when I see you. Suck you off, take your balls
into my mouth, and suck them as well. Would you like that,
Eddie?"

"Yes," he hissed at her. The stream of cum from his tip
was making his fingers slide up and down faster, and his
balls tightened up around his body.

"Come for me, baby. Come shooting that hot cum out of your cock and rub it over your balls." He felt his cock erupt, and when he cried out, she moaned as well. As soon as his hand was covered in his cum, he did just what she'd told him to do and rubbed his balls with the hot juices. When he lay there panting and sticky, he heard her laughter. Edward looked down at himself and felt his anger surge forward.

"What is the meaning of this? You have no right to call here and say those things to me. You're to never call here again for I won't...how did you get this number? This is my personal number, and only friends and associates have it."

"I'm not your friend, Eddie? After making you come so hard all over your desk and papers, you don't think of me as your friend?" He looked at his desk and saw that she was right. Everything there was ruined, and worst yet, so were his clothes. "When I come to see you in an hour, I'm not going to be wearing any panties. Will you bend me over that big desk of yours and fuck me in the ass?"

Edward felt his cock jerk again. As it began to fill and become hard again, he thought of the last time he'd had sex. It had been months. Maybe even the last five years. He could no longer get hard, and this woman had done what hours of porn movies had not. He was ready to go again.

"You're coming here?" He rubbed his cock up and down again as he waited for her to answer. "When?"

Edward wasn't just anxious for her to come to him, but wanted her there now. When she laughed again, the sound a little grating for him, he started to tell her she couldn't. Then she purred again. He nearly came when she moaned too.

"Don't come yet. I want to feel you as you fill my ass." Edward took his hand off his cock, but had to stroke it once more before he finished. "You're going to fuck me hard enough that I come several times before you get to come.

Then when you're finished, I'm going to bite you in the throat and drink from you."

He didn't care so long as he could come again. And the thought of fucking her ass was making him want to take his cock in his hand again. But he didn't. He wanted to please her, and if he came, he might not get to do that again.

When the line went dead, Edward sat there for long minutes trying to decide if it had been a dream or had he really just come all over himself and his desk because a woman had talked dirty to him. Getting up, he went to his door and started to ask his secretary who she had put through. But he didn't. What if the woman had been a figment of his over-tired mind? His desk said otherwise, but he just didn't know. Going to his desk again, he started to sort through what was ruined and wondering how he was going to get fresh copies of the things he really needed. When hands wrapped around his waist from behind, Edward stood very still.

"You're not where I need you to be to fuck me." Her voice, the same as on the phone, tickled his ears. "I'm going to go around you and lean over the desk. Come up from behind me and slam your cock into my ass hard."

Her fingers wrapped around his cock, and he felt himself harden more. He had pulled his underwear up and over his cock but hadn't bothered to button his fly. Edward would have to change, he knew, before he could leave here. But her fingers were working him hard, and he wanted to come just like this. When she pulled away from him, Edward whimpered but turned to see the woman who had brought him such pleasure not an hour ago.

She was lovely. And naked. Edward reached over the desk when she was leaning over it. Her hands braced on the edge and pulled hard on her nipple. Her moan made him want to suckle it into his mouth now.

"Come and fuck me. I need to come after helping you. And when you've brought me, I'll go down on you so I can taste you." Nodding, Edward moved to the other side of his desk and looked at the beautifully shaped ass that was right in front of him. Grabbing her hip with one hand, he fisted his cock with the other. He wasn't sure where to start, but he wanted it all.

"My ass, Eddie, fuck it." He moved his cock into her pussy to get it wet and nearly fucked her there it was so hot, but she ordered him to her ass again, and he moved to the puckered hole there. He was going to enjoy this, he thought.

He pushed past the tight ring with his tip and cried out when it tightened around him. When she moved back, taking more of him in, Edward held onto both her hips to try to slow her. But she was taking him to the root now, and he was moving his hips back and forth fucking her too. When she leaned her head down to his desk, Edward grabbed a handful of her hair and yanked her up. The movement made his cock go incredibly deeper.

"Fuck my pussy with your fingers. Slide along my clit and make me come. When I do, you come too." He did as she instructed and felt the heat of her pussy suck his fingers in. Edward pinched the hard nubbin twice when she tightened her ass around his cock so hard that he felt pained by it. But she screamed out, calling him Eddie and telling him to fuck her harder. Leaning over her body, he fucked her as hard as he could, moving the large oak desk a foot from where it had been. When his climax took him, he sank his teeth into her shoulder to keep from screaming and he tasted blood. Christ, he was going to die from this, he just knew it.

The pain in his wrist startled him, but he was coming again and didn't care what she was doing to hurt him so long as he could do this again and again. As soon as he finished, his body went limp over hers. He nearly fell when she sat up and turned.

"My turn." He was suddenly in his chair, and she was at his cock. He'd never seen her move, but she was sucking his cock so hard and so thoroughly that he again found he didn't care. Edward would never have thought he'd come four times in one month, much less in one hour. When she cupped his balls and gave them a tug, he came again, holding her head over his cock until he emptied himself once again. Edward was too weak and sated to fight her when she tilted his head and licked his throat. When she bit him Edward cried out, but he knew no one would hear him. Christ, she was tearing his throat out.

Edward opened his eyes. He had no idea how long he'd been out, but it was probably only a few seconds. The woman was sitting on his desk with his jacket over her nudity, but her opened legs gave him a perfectly wonderful view of her pussy.

"You want me again?" He nodded, not sure what was going on but wanting to get as much as he could before he really did wake up. "You can have me as much as you want, but I want something in return."

"Anything." And he'd give her anything to be able to fuck her right now. "Tell me what you want and it's yours."

"I want you to invite Stephen to your house. Where, I might as well tell you, I'm going to be staying off and on until this is over." Edward could not believe his luck. This beautiful woman was going to be living with him. He wondered if she'd sleep with him too. Before he could ask her, she smiled at him and rubbed her bare foot over his cock.

"You keep that up and I'm going to come again." She curled her toes around his hardening cock. "I'm never going to survive this if you do this to me daily. I've not had a good erection in years, and here you come into my office and I fucking explode five times."

"You won't." He wasn't sure if she meant he'd never survive or he'd not get to come again. But Edward didn't want to think of either of those options. When she moved her feet to the arms of his chair and leaned back on the desk, he rolled forward and kissed her inner thigh.

Working his way up her leg to her pussy, he thought of several things at once. Her taste, would it be as good as he hoped it would be or better? Edward thought of his lack of a name for her, but she moaned and he forgot about caring. Then she lifted her hips up, and he suckled her clit into his mouth, promptly forgetting the rest of his concerns. And he'd been wrong. She tasted so much better than he'd ever thought she would.

Sucking her pussy, he drank greedily from her. She tasted of him and a sweet nectar that he knew belonged completely to her. Sliding his fingers into her pussy, he moaned when her knees tightened around his head, and he felt her cream running down onto his desk. Christ, this was going to be fantastic.

"Play with my ass." He moved his soaking fingers down to her ass and slid deep. "Oh yeah, that's it. I love my ass to be fucked when I'm being eaten." Her moan made his cock harden again, and he wanted to stand and fuck her this way. But she pulled his head up and looked at him. "I need another man here. I'm going to call in someone to play with us."

52

Edward didn't want to share her, but before he could say anything, a man, as naked as she was, moved into the room. Christ, his cock looked like it was a foot long and at least three inches thick. Edward found he wanted to suck the man's cock just to feel it slide into his throat.

"Stand up and lean onto the desk." The woman moved, and the man was directing him to lean over the desk in the same way that she'd been. When he moved up behind him, Edward felt his cock start to soften until a heavy hand wrapped around him. "No you don't. I'm going to need this later, and if you go all soft on me now, I won't get to have my fun."

The woman moved to get between him and the desk, and she licked his cock as soon as she was on her knees. When she swallowed him down, Edward started fucking her mouth just as the man cupped his balls. As soon as he was leaned over the desk again, he nearly screamed when something entered his ass. The man was fucking him with something smaller than his cock. But the more he rammed it into this ass, the better he was liking it.

"I'm getting you ready to fuck." Edward wasn't sure he'd ever be able to let a man fuck him, but the man's next words had him wanting to try. "You're going to fuck my ass first while I suck off Velvet's pussy. When you come in me, I'm going to fuck you while you fuck her. A threesome with us is going to be amazing."

Edward knew it would. Fucking and being fucked was going to be fucking fantastic. That's when he realized that things had moved. They were in a bedroom he'd never seen before. Velvet was now lying out on the bed and the man was eating her pussy. His ass looked as inviting as her pussy had. Moving up behind him, Edward slammed his cock deep into the man's ass and cried out at the tightness of it.

Nothing in his life had ever felt this good. Edward plowed the man for all he was worth while watching him eat Velvet's pussy. Christ, he hoped he'd never wake from this.

Chapter 4

Stephen watched her sleep. He knew that she was healing much faster than anyone thought she would, but he'd been giving her more and more of his blood over the past few hours to hurry the process up. He kept telling himself that it was because he wanted to get her as far from him as possible, but really he wanted to see her eyes again. Samuel had told him he could see the world in them and he wanted to see if that was true. Stephen had a feeling he would be able to see more.

The meeting yesterday and again early this morning had not gone as planned. First of all, they were trying their best to piss him off about this council position. He didn't want it for any number of reasons.

"But most of all, it's because if I take it, it might require me to follow some of the rules that I think are stupid." His voice echoed in the room, but he enjoyed speaking. Stephen didn't want to think that he was sharing his frustrations with his mate, but knew that's just what he was doing. He leaned back into his chair and looked at her.

"This will never work. You will begin to hate me after a while because of what I am. I don't mean a vampire, but the bastard that I am." He shifted on the seat, uncomfortable with his own words. "I can be ruthless when need be, but I've been known to be a sort of nice guy. But you'll see me for what I am. All of me. I drink from a bag now, not because I think humans should never be used as a source of food, but because I simply don't want to bother."

He got up and went to the window to look out. The light on the yard showed that it was home to two deer and a small rodent. They ignored each other for the most part. One of the deer lifted her head as he watched, and he wondered if one of the wolves had startled her. When the deer both took off toward the woods, he smiled when one of the wolves chased them. He knew that they'd never kill one of them, but the need to run was born in them. He thought of Velvet December.

"She's gunning for me. And if she finds out that you're my mate, she'll stop at nothing to harm you. It's why you have to leave here." Three more wolves moved through the light, but these were moving as though they were searching, not hunting. "I've had to find extra patrols, as well as update the security."

"Because of me." Stephen turned, startled by the voice behind him. She still lay on the bed, but she was staring at him. "Is it because of me?"

"Yes. No. I would have done it anyway, but this expedited things a little." She didn't move and neither did he. He wasn't even sure he could. "Are you hurting?"

"Yes." He waited for her to explain, but she turned her head away from him, and he felt sorry for that. "I'll leave as soon as I can. I'm not sure how badly I've been beaten to shit this time, but I'll go when I can."

Moving toward the chair, Stephen sat down before speaking. "I don't think you need to leave right away. But you will have to. I don't want you here. As it is right now, Velvet doesn't know where I live, but it won't be long."

She didn't speak again, and he felt badly about that. He didn't have a clue as to why, but he did. Instead of leaving as he knew he should, he settled in the chair to wait her out. He had a great deal of practice at waiting for people to speak first, and this slip of a human was going to be easy. Closing his eyes, he decided to rest while she sulked.

Stephen opened his eyes. He had no idea how long he'd slept, but he knew it was longer than he'd meant to. Lately, he'd not been resting as well as he should have been, and that was why he'd slept for so long, he told himself. Not since the woman had...he looked at the bed for several seconds before he realized what he was seeing. She was gone. And someone had made the bed. Getting up, he moved to the door, reaching for her as he went. Nothing.

"Mother fuck." The door opened just as he was reaching for it, and there stood Kasen. He looked as startled as Stephen felt. When Stephen looked at the tray in his hand, he realized he was bringing him his morning food.

"Where is she?" Kasen looked to the stairs before looking at him. "When did she get up? And why did no one wake me?"

"She came down several hours ago, sire. Miss Kelley said that you were resting and that you'd given her permission to leave. She said you insisted on it." His heart started pounding with the thought of her leaving him...here. "I have sent all manner of food with her as she didn't seem to have—"

"She's gone?" Kasen took a step back and nodded. "When? Mother fuck. She's not well enough to be out gallivanting around like she's invincible. And I did not give her permission to leave. I said that...I don't remember what

57

I said to her, but I most certainly did not give her permission to leave."

"I was not aware that she required it." He glared at Leith as she landed on the tray that Kasen held. "Did you not tell her just this morning that she would need to leave? That she was not wanted here?"

Stephen moved past his day walker and to the stairs as he answered her. "I told her the truth. She is not wanted here, but that didn't mean I wanted her to get out there and get herself killed. Why the hell aren't you with her anyway? I thought you were her great protector."

"Because she asked me to tell you something." Stephen nearly fell down the last three steps. Turning slowly, he looked at the tiny woman. She didn't look any happier to give him the message than he was to receive it. But when she moved past him and toward his office, he followed.

"There is snow everywhere. Did you see it?" He glanced out the window as he sat, not bothering to comment on her question. "It will be cold as the moon rises higher in the sky. I tried to get her to take more blankets when she left, but she said that you'd more than likely accuse her of being a thief, and she said she had enough on her plate right now without adding jail time to it."

"I would not have begrudged her extra blankets." He huffed at Leith as he continued. "I told her I was a bastard. She might have heard me."

"I told her." That startled him to silence. "When you were speaking to her, I was there. I didn't think that you'd mind that she had the information you were giving her while she slept."

He hadn't meant for her to know what a bastard he... Stephen looked at the faerie when she smiled. "You told her everything. Even what I thought about myself."

"I did. Did you mind?"

He found that he did. Leaning back in his chair, he tried to think how to find out if she was all right without making himself look like a fool.

Leith sat on his blotter and looked up at him. "It does not feel right, does it, my lord? To have someone that should mean the world to you to be out in the cold, alone. Would you like her message?"

Nodding, he thought about telling her no. Getting up, he went to the window again and saw her footprints going toward the woods. He could follow her. Reaching for the man in charge of his brigade of wolves, he asked Jimmy if he knew where she had gone.

She is holed up in a cave about four miles from here. I'm not sure how she made it, but she did. Stubborn little thing. The seriousness of his voice made Stephen know that he hadn't found any humor in her stubbornness. *I have three of my men watching her now. I don't think she'll be going anywhere for a while. Oh, and did you know that she can talk to us? I mean communicate with us on the same level that only supers can?*

No. But nothing she does right now should surprise me. She walked right by me without waking me. How the hell did she do that? He reached for her again to hit the same hard wall. *And why the hell can she block me? I've given her enough blood to turn her, and yet she can still keep me out of her head.*

Fuck her. He was sure Jimmy meant in the physical sense of the word, but he was in no mood for someone to give him advice on his wayward mate. Moving to the door, he saw his friend standing there pulling on an old shirt. Jimmy looked like he was going to say more, but Stephen held up his hand.

"Save it. Just take me to her and I'll deal with her." When Jimmy only crossed his arms over his chest, Stephen felt his beast rise. He should have known that it wouldn't do him any good. Jimmy just threw back his head and laughed at him.

"You think that'll work on her? I'm thinking not. When we were following her through the woods, she stopped and turned to us. Looked at the others before settling that glare on me. Asked me what the fuck I was doing." Jimmy moved past him and into the house, leaving Stephen no choice but to follow or stand there looking stupid...or in this case, stupider.

Kasen was asking Jimmy what he wanted to eat, and Leith was sitting next to a tiny plate that had several flowers on it. She was nibbling on one when he sat down. The urge to flick her away was great, but Stephen had a feeling that she'd hurt him in ways that he would feel for years, if not his entire life. She seemed to know what he was thinking and laughed at him.

"You have never taken her message. Would you like it now?" Stephen nodded. "She said to tell you to leave her alone. That she has enough overbearing dickheaded men in her life, and she does not need another one that thinks he can control her. Also, she said that if you come to find her, she will...I believe she meant this in a way that is not good. She said that if you come to find her that she will 'fuck you up.'"

"I'm sure you're right." He watched as Kasen sat a large platter of food in front of Jimmy and wondered briefly how he'd made it so quickly. Then he remembered the girl and looked at Leith. "Can you tell me who is chasing her and why?"

"It is as you think. Her stepfather. I'm not sure what that term is, but that is what she calls him. His name is Edward Barron." Stephen felt his world pinpoint on the name.

Christ, he knew him. "I see that his name has sparked a memory?"

"He's a man that I deal with sometimes. His firm does advertising, and when I have some new product that I want to sell, he's the firm I go to. You say that he's her stepfather? And that would be a term used to call someone who has married your blood mother but is not your real father." Leith nodded as she finished the second flower. "I don't know how old Clar is, but I'm betting she's older than twenty-one. What does he want with her?"

"I am not sure. But she mentioned that he will rot in his own juices before she lets him hit her again. Why would he hit someone as lovely as her?" Stephen didn't know but he was willing to find out and show the man what hitting his mate could get him. "My lord, she is not well enough to defend herself against the elements and someone who may want to harm her. No matter that we've heated the cave up for her, she is still out where she can be hurt. Also, she is older than that, my lord. I believe her to be twenty and ten."

"I'm hoping that when Jimmy here finishes eating me out of house and home, he'll take me to her." He looked at Leith as he finished. "Unless you know where she is."

"The same place as before." Stephen stood up and willed himself to her...to hell with all this waiting around. If she got hurt, it would be his fault. He really didn't know how it would be his fault, but it just felt as if it would be.

Clar was standing near the fire when he walked into the cave.

"Are you that stupid?" He looked at her, then behind him when she spoke. "Yes you, you moron. I told you that I was fine. And you told me that you didn't want me around. Why on earth would you be here now when I've done just as you asked?"

"I told you to wait until you were well." She sat down, and he decided that enough was enough. "Gather what you are going to need and I'll take you back to my house. This is just stupid for you to be living in a cave when there is no earthly reason for you to be here."

"There's plenty of reasons, none of which I care to share with you. And as for the stuff I took from your home, it was just food. That guy, Kasen, said it would go bad if I didn't take it, as neither of you eat food." She cocked her head at him. "Do you drink from that nice man? If so, I would think you'd be a little nicer, what with his blood in your body and all."

"I do not drink from my help. There's a law forbidding…I'm not going to explain the laws of my kind to you. I asked you to gather your things and we'll go back to my house. Get with it; or would you like for me to do it for you?" It was a threat, and they both knew it. But she only sat there warming her hands over the blazing fire. "I'm speaking to you."

"No, you're ordering me. And you didn't ask me to do anything. Again, you ordered. I don't have to listen to you because you're not…I don't remember what you called it, and you're most definitely not my father. Step or otherwise." She frowned, then looked up at him. "Mate. I'm not your mate. Why I would want to be anyway is beyond me."

"Because it affords you things that your kind can only dream of." He wanted her, he realized. All her back talking him and her stubbornness made him want to pull her to his body and then press her against any hard surface to plow deep within her. "Would you please come back to my house with me?"

She didn't move, and for some reason he was more impressed than pissed off. But she still could not stay here. Not alone and certainly not with Velvet walking around. He wanted to reason with her. Wanted to explain things to her, but decided he was not changing his ways just because she was his supposed mate.

"Get your things now and we'll go back. It'll be too hot for me to be out soon, and I'd just as soon not fry just because you have your panties in a twist about my manners." She tossed another log on the fire and said nothing. "I know you can hear me. Now do as I say."

"Fuck off." Stephen felt his temper rise, but she stood up then, and he could see that while she was lovely in the first place, when her temper was high, she was positively gorgeous. The blast of magic nearly took his breath away, and it did take him off his feet. She looked as surprised as he felt. When he started to stand, she lifted her hand again, and he felt the pressure on his chest start to hurt. She was doing this, and neither of them, it appeared, knew how.

"Get out." He shook his head but didn't move. "I mean it. I don't know how the fuck this is happening, and I don't know if I can control it. So unless you want to be my guinea pig, I suggest you get out while the getting is good."

"A vampire is looking to hurt me, and in turn she might find you. If she does, she'll have no problem using you to get to me." Clar frowned. "You have to come back to my house to keep her from finding you."

"And just why would you give a shit if she killed me?" He had no answer for her question, so didn't bother. "Just as I thought. I'm better off on my own. If someone finds me, her or someone else, I won't have to worry if you get your throat cut. And one or both of them just might do it if I don't first."

"I know your stepfather." She took a step back, and he felt the pressure on his chest lighten, so he stood up but didn't move toward her. "He and I worked together on a few projects that I have in the works. I had no idea who he was to you until Leith told me. Why is he trying to find you?"

"He thinks because I didn't do as he told me, I owe him somehow. Now that I think about it, I can see how the two of you would get along. You're both cut from the same cloth."

Stephen felt his anger burst forward but didn't act on it. It wasn't her fault that she didn't know that he was going to cut ties with the man as soon as he could. But she should have had more faith in him.

"Why?" When she spoke, he looked at her as she stood there. Her hands were planted firmly on her hips, and her legs spread, the stance of a warrior, and he loved it. Taking a step toward her, he stopped when she raised her hand again. "Why should I have more faith in you?"

He stared at her for several seconds when he realized she'd read his mind. "That's somewhat rude, don't you think? Reading my mind when you have me blocked from yours. How are you doing that anyway? I've given you my blood; your mind should be an open book to me."

"And what do you plan to do with it? My mind, I mean. Have me go to meetings with you so I can tell you what people really think of you? Or did you want me to manipulate their mind so that they see things your way?" She put her finger on her chin as if she were thinking on it. Then when she snapped her finger as if she'd figured it out, her grin did not reassure him. "I know. You want me to bring you victims so you can have your way with them as you drain them. Whatever the reason, you're not getting in.

I don't know how I can do half the crap I can since the day my mom's car was high-jacked, but there you have it. I can block you and anyone else, and fuck you for wanting to control that part of me."

"I don't." She snorted, and he took a step toward her. The sun was pulling at him, not badly yet, but it would soon be necessary for him to leave. And he was taking her with him. His next step brought him to within touching distance, but he didn't touch her. "Will you please come back to my house with me? I want to make sure that you're safe."

"No." He reached for her then and felt the connection almost as soon as his fingers brushed against her skin. But in the next second, less probably, he was sailing across the cave and hitting the stone behind him. His last thought was, *fuck, she is strong.*

~~~

Samuel was just putting Kendal, his precious son, down for a nap when he felt someone enter his mind. He thought it was Stephen, but as soon as the woman spoke, he was glad then that he'd not said the glib remark to him about having a mate. He could feel her anger the moment he let her in.

That vampire is hurt. Can you send someone to get him? I've tried to reach out to the wolves, but I can't get the one in charge to answer me yet. Samuel moved down the stairs after telling the nurse he was leaving the house and that Kennedy would be back shortly. *Are you listening to me?*

Yes. I have someone here, and he requires a good deal more of my attention than you do at the moment. Where is Stephen? She told him in her home.

He banged his head on the wall when this new thing got the better of me. He could hear her frustration, but he was no less confused. *For some reason I can do this new bit with my mind. I only meant to shove him away, but he flew out like I'd hit him with a rocket. He hit his head. Pretty hard, I'm guessing, for it to crack it like it did. Had you asked me, I would have thought the stone would have given before his hard head would have.*

Samuel decided right then and there that he liked this girl. She had a sense of humor that made him smile even though things were very serious. *If by your home you mean the cave you'd been in when we found you, I'm on my way. And I will contact Jimmy too to have him meet me there. Don't hurt him.*

I won't. She was snappish too, and he found that to be as funny as anything. *You know, you people are getting on my last nerve. All I did was save my friend and him. You'd think he'd be a little more inclined to do as I asked instead of...* When she stopped talking Samuel was suddenly afraid. Shifting quickly, he moved toward the cave, reaching for Jimmy at the same time.

We're close, but we can't go to her. Not yet at any rate. There's enough power coming from this place that I'm afraid to let my men go near it. Samuel told Jimmy it was the girl and she was having some issues about controlling it. *No shit. I think there are about ten kinds of shit going on in there right now, and I'm not risking my neck to find out what it is.*

I'm on my way. Hopefully by the time I get there she'll have it calmed down. Oh, and she knocked Stephen on his ass. She said she cracked his head open. Jimmy laughed and he joined him. *I hope she does it a few more times while she's at it.*

Me too. Samuel could see Jimmy and three wolves standing near a stand of trees. He could feel the magic coming from the opening, but like them, didn't move to go inside. Reaching out to the woman, he said her name softly.

Clar, we're here. Can you calm your magic down so we can come inside? She didn't answer him right away, and he started to speak to her again. But just then she staggered out of the cave opening and fell to her knees. They all rushed toward her at once, but stopped when she looked at them.

"I healed him. I'm not...I think I'm going to be sick." She started to stand up but fell back down onto her knees and leaned over. As she threw up twice, Jimmy went into the cave. Samuel wanted to shift to care for her, but if she really healed Stephen, he might not be too happy to see a naked man standing next to his mate. No matter how much Stephen didn't want her, she was still the one that would have him murder his friends if they fucked around with her. And that included helping her if he was pissed enough.

Jimmy came out of the cave with Stephen. He was standing on his own, but he looked pale, and there was blood on his shirt. As soon as he saw Clar, he moved toward her with a cautious step. Good, Samuel thought, maybe he'd live another day.

"I'm taking you back to my house." She stood up and staggered slightly when Stephen spoke. "I don't want to hear how you'll be fine and dandy. Because, frankly, I have no idea what the fuck that even means. But I'm tired and hungry. So unless you want me to take you into the cave and fuck you while I feed from you, I suggest you do as I say."

"You try it, buster, and I'll hurt you again." She moved back when Stephen moved forward, and Samuel wanted to step between the two of them just to keep the peace. But he was enjoying the fact that she would stand up to someone as powerful as Stephen.

"You'll do as I say, or so help me..." Stephen looked at him, and Samuel wanted to tell him that he might be better off leaving her there for now and trying a calmer approach. But whatever he might have been going to say was cut off when a part of the stone opening to the cave shattered.

It happened so quickly that he wasn't sure how he was tossed to the ground. One second he was standing next to Jimmy, and the next, he was laying on the dirt with someone on top of him. He tried to move and heard a harsh voice tell him to be still. It was Stephen.

"Someone is firing at us." Samuel started to raise his head but was shoved back down. "Do you fucking want to get killed? Lay the fuck still while I try to figure this out."

"I want to breathe if you don't mind." Stephen shifted, and Samuel could see then. Clar was standing, but she seemed to have a glow around her. That was when he realized she had a protective shield around her and the rest of them. Stephen stood up then and looked around while still in the shield. Christ, Samuel thought, they looked so right together that he was stunned.

"I can't hear them." Stephen nodded at Clar when she spoke. He saw Stephen whisper in her ear just before he put his hands on her shoulders. She seemed to glow more, and Samuel knew that he was helping her. "There are three of them. One of them is younger by far than the others. The oldest...a man about forty...shot at us. He is disappointed that he couldn't kill me. The middle man thinks that this is just going to get him back in jail. The youngest is...he's aroused because he got to shoot at a vampire."

Stephen held onto Clar's shoulders as she continued. Samuel knew that he was hyping up her abilities and was amazed by it. He wondered how much further she could read peoples' minds when the shield was lowered. Samuel sat there for several seconds trying to wrap his mind around what just happened.

"Will you please come to my house with me now?" Stephen started pacing when Clar shook her head. "I don't want to have to make you go with me, but I will if you don't try to see reason. Someone is out to kill you. Can't you see that?"

"I can see a great deal. What I don't understand is why you give a shit." Stephen stopped pacing and stared at her as she continued. "You said yourself that you don't want me. You've even gone so far as to tell others that you don't. So again, I ask you, why do you care what happens to me? Because I gotta tell you, I'm completely confused."

Stephen pulled her into his arms. The kiss he gave her was searing and heated. Samuel watched as Stephen pulled her body to his and wrapped her around him. In seconds they were gone, and Samuel let out a long, slow breath. Christ, he felt the need from his friend as if it were his own. He looked at Jimmy, who looked just as stunned.

"Now what?" Samuel shrugged. "Christ, I don't know about you, but I want to go and find my mate."

So did Samuel. And right fucking now. He stood up and shook the snow that had begun to fall off his coat. Taking off toward his home, he was astounded at his own need. If the couple that had just left them were half as needy as he was, he actually felt sorry for them. Or not. They'd likely kill each other before they finished. But they'd have a great time while they were at it.

Chapter 5

Edward woke with a start. He had no idea where he was, nor did he know why he was so sore. Moving as quickly as his body would allow him, he sat up. Realization hit him like a ball bat between the eyes. He'd fucked and been fucked by a man. Several times, if memory served him. Looking around the overdone room, he stood up and moved to the bathroom. This room was no easier on his eyes than the one he'd just left.

The red toilet and countertop made him think of blood. The tile floor, nearly the same color as the others, had black grout between each of the two–by–two inch slabs of clay. The shower stall was a flat black color, and the glass surrounding it looked like it was shattered. But when he touched it, he could see that it was the pattern of it rather than it being broken. The towels, two of which hung on the bar that was on the shower and the smaller one at the sink, were also black. It matched the room beyond well, as it too was done up in velvet of the same color. He looked at himself in the mirror above the sink.

He looked like he'd gone several rounds with a fighter and had come up short. Very short. He turned his head to the right and saw that he'd been cut a few times. But upon closer inspection, he could see that they were punctures, not cuts. Edward remembered that at one point he'd been bitten, and his mind skittered away from that thought. Reaching into the shower, he turned the water on, half expecting it to come out black or that deep red, but it sprayed out plain water. As he was already naked, Edward stepped into the spray.

His ass was so sore when he rubbed the cloth over it that he had to grab the wall for support. He knew that the man who had violated him had been large, and knew that as much as he wanted to forget the entire thing, there was no way he'd be able to so long as he was this sore. He washed his body four times before turning off the taps. Standing there shivering slightly, he reached for the towel, hoping that it was as clean as he now was. The knock at the door started a cry from him.

"My lord, I have breakfast for you. Where would you like for me to set it up?" The man on the other side of the door cleared his throat as he continued. "If I may be so bold, sire, I have brought you some pain medications as well. In addition, there are clothes for you to put on."

Wrapping the towel around his waist, Edward walked out of the bathroom and stared at the large man standing there. When he took a step toward him, Edward moved back. The man seemed to understand and took a few steps back as well. Pointing to the clothing on the bed, he moved to the small table in the corner.

"Where are they?" He hadn't meant to ask, but he needed to know if he could make a clean break. "And how do I get home?"

"They are resting, my lord. As for you leaving, we were told you would be residing here for a time." The man lifted covers off two plates, and Edward felt his mouth water. If it tasted only half as good as it smelled, he was going to devour the entire thing. Moving toward the table, he thought about what the man had said.

"I'm not staying here. I don't even know where here is. I'm assuming I didn't drive here." The butler or whatever he was shook his head as he poured orange juice into a glass from a large carafe. "Can you call me a cab or something?"

"I cannot. Shall you require something else to eat, sire?" Edward told him no and asked again about transportation. "They have said you will stay. It is not possible for me to go against the mistress's wishes. And if you were smart, sire, you would not either."

After the man left, Edward looked at the food. There was so much of it, he wondered who the man thought he was feeding. There were ten sausage links, as well as thick slices of ham. Several eggs had to have been broken to make the omelet that took up his entire plate. And the coffee smelled like heaven. Biting into the croissant that was still warm, Edward picked up his fork. He was nearly finished with the meal when he thought of what the woman had said to him before he'd fallen asleep.

"I need for you to get me Stephen. I have a few people out looking for him, but I want you to invite him to your house when we go back there." She'd moved over his body again, nipping at his flesh as she made her way to his cock again. "When you have him where I want him, I will give you a great gift. Would you like that?"

"Christ, yes. Suck me again." He had felt the man behind him, and when he moved down his body, Edward had moaned. Now all he could think about was that the man had forced himself onto him. Then, all he'd been able to think about was him taking his cock again. But neither of them had touched him as they moved down the bed and off it. When Velvet had told him to sleep, he did. Edward wondered if he'd ever be the same after this.

Finishing the meal completely, he stood up. The butler had made the bed while he'd been in the shower, and Edward sat down on it. Exhaustion pulled at him, but he needed to get home. If nothing else, he had to call in to his office to make sure that no one was slacking off. Heading down the stairs, he made his way to the kitchen, where he heard voices.

"Sire. Are you finished with your repast?" Edward nodded, and one of the women standing there left the room. "Do you need something else? You should drink more liquids. You'll feel better if you do."

"I don't want anything to drink. What I want is to leave." The man handed him a glass of orange juice, and before he could think to splash it into the man's face, Edward drank it down in one gulp. Handing the glass back to him, Edward walked to the door.

"Sire, I would not if I were you. The mistress was quite firm about you staying until she releases you." Edward turned to look at the man. "She will be most unpleasant when she finds you gone from here when she rises."

"Rises? You've said that before. What do you mean?" The man looked a little frightened, and Edward had a feeling he didn't want to know the answer to his question. For that matter, he wished he could forget the entire night. Moving to the door again, he froze when the man behind him spoke.

"A vampire must rest during the day, my lord. And her minion, Ted, will rest with her as well. In the event she gets hungry during her rest, he will be there for her." Edward didn't want to think about all the times she'd bitten him. He'd tried his best to tell himself she was giving him love bites, as had Ted. But the butler continued before he could try to come up with a better reason why she was resting. "She will rise when the sun is gone, sire, and when she does, she will be most angry with you if you are not in her bed again."

Edward was surprised to find the door unlocked when he turned the handle. There was no way he was staying in this madhouse. Moving down the three little stairs, he felt the sun on his face and wondered why it burned just a little. Moving down the long drive, he walked along the sidewalk, keeping his mind purposely blank. All he thought about was his left foot, then his right one going forward. There was no way he'd just left a house of vampires.

By the time he was able to hail a cab, he was sweating. His body ached in places he was sure he didn't have a name for. And when he had the cabbie wait while someone from the house came out with money, he was shaking so hard that he could hardly stand. It took his own butler four tries to get him into the house. When he was wrapped up in his bed, several blankets all around him, Edward was afraid that he'd been poisoned. By the time he was drifting off, Edward was wishing for death.

~~~

Clar tried to pull away from the man who held her, but Stephen wasn't having it. He was touching her everywhere, and she both wanted him to let her go and to take her. When something soft touched her back, she yanked his hair up and looked him in the eyes. What she saw there made her pause.

"I want you." She didn't say anything, but didn't pull away from him either. "Let me take you the way I want, and I'll give you so much pleasure you'll never want anything else."

"And then what? You'll toss me to the street again? Or will you turn me over to my stepfather? You're a great deal like him. Did you know that? Ordering people around as if you're the king of the world." Stephen moved slightly, and she could feel his cock right at her entrance. When she looked down her body, she could see that she was as naked as he was. "Do you plan to rape me too?"

"You will not think it's rape when I finish." He moved into her slightly, and she moaned. "Do you want more? Would you like for me to go deeper? I can."

"I want you to stop this." His grin told her that he didn't believe her any more than she did. "You don't want me." This time when he rocked into her, she felt herself stretch and fill with him.

"I think we can both agree that I do want you. Badly." He moved again, this time moving out before sliding back into her. "You're very wet and hot. I feel you around my cock like a hot furnace."

Her feet moved on their own, wrapping around his calves. "You don't want me. You want to fuck me. Get off me."

His laughter made her angry, but he moved again, moving deep within her. She cried out. It wasn't as if she were a virgin, but he was much bigger than she was used to. When she suddenly straddled him and he was on his back, she looked down at where they were connected as only a man and woman could be. She moved, just enough to try and get off him, when he put his hands on her hips and held her still.

"You move too much, love, and this will be over long before we get started." His voice had grown husky, and she looked into his face. She knew a couple of other vampires and had learned that when their eyes were dark, bloodied like his were now, they were either very pissed or hungry.

"Are you going to bite me?" He nodded and pulled her hips forward enough that she moaned. "I don't want to have sex with you. Well, I do, but that's not all you want, is it?"

"No. I want to feed from you as well. But there is so much more I want than sex, too. I want to taste your pussy as well. Would you enjoy that?" She nodded, then shook her head. "Ah, so it sounds enjoyable but not with me doing it. Is that it?"

"I want to come. Then I want you to let me go." She rode him, moving up and down his cock as if she were actually riding a horse. "I need to come, but not at the expense of you thinking this will continue."

"If you let me bite you, I'm sure you'll change your mind." She was afraid of that as well, but moved off him and stood. His cock was soaking wet and straining from his groin. As much as she wanted to finish what he'd started, she didn't want him to own her. And if they mated or whatever it was, she had no doubt he would think he did.

His fingers wrapped around his cock while she stood there, and her mouth watered. He was using her juices to masturbate, and she wanted to taste the pearl of cream at the tip of his cock. Taking another step back, she watched him as he continued to pleasure himself.

"Come here, Clar. I want to come all over you." She shook her head even as she moved toward the bed again. "Take me into your mouth. Take me and I'll drink from your pussy while you do."

She wanted to. Her body ached to do just what he wanted. When his hand touched her thigh, she turned toward him and he slid his fingers into her pussy. While he fisted his cock faster and faster, his other hand played with her clit and slid in and out of her quicker and quicker.

"Come here." She moved toward him, her body no longer listening to her. When she was near his head, he lifted her up and settled her pussy over his mouth. She looked down her body as he ate her and felt her climax rushing forward. Clar leaned forward and took his cock into her mouth and moaned around him. He tasted like paradise.

Clar rode his mouth. She needed to come so badly now that she would do anything to feel it happen. When Stephen slid his fingers into her ass, she nearly told him to stop, but he growled at her, and she felt it race along her body like a live wire. Then his cock erupted in her mouth, and she swallowed him.

"Christ," she heard him say as he fucked her mouth. Over and over she tasted his cum and cupped his balls when he seemed to be slowing. She wanted it all, every last drop of him. When he rolled her to her back, still fucking her mouth, she grabbed his ass just as her own release took her. Clar screamed around his cock even as she felt his teeth sink into her clit.

Her world didn't shatter so much as imploded. Her mind skittered to a stop, and she was sure her heart did as well. As soon as her climax started to slow, he would suck hard on her and bring her again. All the while his fingers danced in both her pussy and ass. She had so many climaxes in a few short minutes that she was weak with them. Finally, she begged him to stop by reaching into his mind and telling him she'd had enough.

Clar felt herself being moved. She knew that he was lifting her up, but she was settled back on the bed so quickly that she wasn't sure if she'd dreamed it. When he said her name, she had to will her eyes to open, they were so heavy.

"Are you okay?" She shook her head and heard him laugh as she closed her eyes again. "You'll need to stay awake for just a few more minutes, love."

"I want you to take me back to my home." She didn't think he answered her when she felt a blanket cover her. "Okay, I'll rest for a minute, but I'm not staying here. I don't want to be your mate."

"It's a little too late for that." She thought so too but didn't say anything to him. "Clar, can you please tell me you won't leave me if I leave you here to rest?"

"I can't promise you anything." Yawning, she thought she heard him curse but wasn't sure. "I'm going to leave here as soon as I rest up. You having sex with me changes nothing."

"It changes everything, I'm afraid. And you being stubborn about this isn't going to mean anything once you realize how much you belong to me now." She yawned again before saying anything. Her body had never been this relaxed and sated after sex.

"I don't think I'd be able to be this satisfied if I decided to have sex again." He growled, and she made a mental note to remember that he didn't like her talking about other men. "You'll find some other blood sucker to live with you. I have to keep away from my stepfather. So if you could give me a couple of days' head start I'd be ever so grateful."

Sleep took her. Not a gentle roll into sleep, but where she just felt it take her. Much like one of the many climaxes that he'd given her. When she felt the bed shift, she felt herself roll toward a great weight and knew that he slept with her. She smiled.

Stephen was wrapped around her when she woke up sometime later. His body was big, but not crushing like one other guy she'd slept with. His was...well, she thought, like a warm blanket, but didn't want to get that cozy with him. It took her several tries before she finally had to move into his mind and try to make him leave her. But when she entered his mind, she wished she'd just lain there.

Someone was going to bury him alive. The memory of it and the person who had done it was right there and she let it play out. He'd been accused of something, and his sentence was to be put to the earth to never rise again. She felt his horror at the sentencing and wanted to hold onto him when the man standing before him asked if he had anything to say.

"Don't do this, brother. Please. I didn't touch your wife. I swear to you." The man shook his head and they both looked at the woman who stood crying nearby. "I never touched her. She lies to save herself."

"She is my wife. She would never lie to me." But the look on the man's face made Clar think that he didn't really believe his words either. "You have lain with her and now she is carrying your child. What do you have to say for yourself?"

"It is not my child. I never touched her. You know that. We cannot father children with anyone but our mates." The man slapped him, and she felt herself, with him, tumble back. As he lay there staring up at the man, someone threw heavy chains around him, and she too felt the weight of them. The woman stood over Stephen just as the hole was being filled with dirt.

"You think you're so smart. And now you're going to pay for ignoring me." She spit on his face, and Clar put her hand to her cheek to see if it were real. A hand touched hers just as she pulled her dry hand away. It was Stephen and he was awake, staring at her as he had the woman standing over them...him.

"She told him that she was having my child. That I had forced her into having sex with me so that I could cockle him." Clar nodded as Stephen looked down at her. "You should know that I'd never do that to a woman. Human or otherwise."

"What happened when you were released?" She watched his face shutter closed and reached up to touch his cheek. "Tell me. Tell me what happened when you got free."

He got up from the bed and moved toward the window. There was light coming through the drawn curtain, but he didn't seem to see it. She knew that he was still there, back when he'd been buried, and knew that for as long as he lived he'd never rest where it was completely dark again.

"I clawed my way out of the ground when I heard someone call my name. I didn't know who it was at the time. I had thought it was Clive, my brother, having a change of heart. But it was Vinnie…Vicente McIntyre, my friend. He had not heard from me in a while and came to find me."

"How long?" He looked at her but said nothing as he pulled on his pants. Clar pulled the sheet up over her nudity, suddenly embarrassed to be caught like she was. "How long were you underground?"

"Seventy years. Not long in the life of a vampire, but long enough for me to plan out my revenge. I was starved when I was pulled free, and nearly killed the great dragon when he helped me." Clar wondered if Stephen was using a strange reference in calling this Vinnie person or if he actually was a dragon. Before she could ask, he continued.

"He let me feed from his strong blood, but it wasn't enough. I needed…I was in a blood lust. A need so deep that I hurt him." She didn't say anything as he pulled on his shirt and sat down. But she did get up and reach for the shirt that was on the floor. Hers was in tatters, and she'd not even realized he'd done it.

As he sat there not saying anything, she dressed. There was no point in talking to him now, she could see that, and moved toward the door when she had on her jeans. He was suddenly behind her, pressing her against the door.

"Don't you want to hear the rest? You've touched my mind enough to see what frightens me badly enough that I need a night light like a small child." He turned her then, and she could see the anger in his eyes. "He buried me there. Near the barn where we'd played as children. A place where my father had raised horses for the noblemen of the village. He told me he'd leave no marker other than a stake in the ground to show what sort of animal I was. Then I was freed. Do you know what I did then?"

"You killed him. And his wife." Stephen nodded and lifted her up so that they were eye to eye. "You're hurting me."

"I ripped his throat out as he lay there resting. Tore it out and spit it back into his face. His blood was bitter, cold as he was. His mate, however, I took more time with. I pulled her free of her resting place and dragged her out into the sun. It took me longer than I had wanted, but I had her staked to the ground, pikes of wood driven through her hands and feet, spread out so that nothing would be untouched by the sun as it blazed over us. As she burned, her body peeling from her bones, I heard someone screaming. I looked up to see a child running to me, my mother just behind him. And when they reached me, do you know what I did? I killed it. Slashed out my hand and tore it in two. He was dead before he touched the earth."

"You killed their child." He nodded and buried his face into her neck. She could feel his hot breath there as his tongue licked a path along her vein. "Don't do this. You'll hurt me if you do."

Lifting his head, he looked at her, and she felt his anger pour over her. "I should have left you in the cave. I should have stayed away. This is what you get for spying on someone as powerful as me."

He tilted her head and tore into her throat. She cried out as he drank from her. The pleasure and the pain were almost too much. When he lifted her up, she felt his cock at her entrance as he ripped her pants from her. When he entered her, hard and deep, Clar cried out again. This time he didn't give her any pleasure, but came in her almost as soon as he took her.

Clar held onto his shoulders as he fed from her. Her body was weak with it when he finally lifted his head. When he staggered back from her, she held onto the door. There was no way she'd let him touch her again after this. As he fell to the floor, she stood there watching him, and when she was sure he was out, Clar staggered to his closet. Taking out the first thing she touched, she grabbed a shirt and a pair of his pants. They would both be too big for her, but she had no choice at the moment. When she was dressed, she opened his drawers until she found some socks and went to the door again. Looking back at him, she thought of how much pain he was in.

"You are no better than the man who locked you beneath the ground. You took something that didn't belong to you. If you come near me again, I'll take your head off and never think another thing about it." Clar went out of the room and was nearly down the stairs when she realized she had nowhere to go.

Kasen, a man she remembered from before, was standing in the kitchen when she entered. He didn't say anything but pulled her to the chair and sat her down. Clar had no idea what she might look like, but was sure that it was frightening. As he sat a glass of something in front of her, he also handed her a wet cloth.

"You must clean up, my lady, or you'll frighten anyone who would happen to see you." Nodding, she rubbed it onto her face and stared at the bloodied rag when she looked at it. "Come now, clean up. I'll get you fed, then find you somewhere to stay."

"I can't stay in the cave again. He knows where that is." He only nodded and picked up the phone.

Chapter 6

Kennedy didn't know what to make of the woman. She sat as still as a statue and never so much as looked at anyone when they said her name. When someone walked into the room, she looked at Brigitte and shook her head.

"'Tis shock, my lady. I would imagine one such as her would be shocked by the events of the day." Kennedy wasn't sure what she'd meant by "such as her" but nodded. It had been a shock for her to see the woman when Samuel had brought her there.

"He drank from her. And if my nose is right, they mated as well." Brigitte sat a glass of juice in front of Clar and then left the room. Kennedy sat near the girl and wondered what else had happened to her that would make her look this way.

Her hair was hanging in a long knot. Not a messy one that indicated that she'd not brushed it, but it looked as if she'd tied it into a knot at the back of her head. Her face was pale, but she thought it was due more to her heritage than anything else. And her eyes, when she'd looked at her, had seemed haunted, vacant too. Kennedy wanted to find Stephen and murder him in his sleep.

KATHI S. BARTON

"I don't want you to do that." Kennedy sat back in her chair when Clar continued. "First of all, it will do you no good to murder him. What's done is done. And secondly…well, secondly, he's your friend and you'd regret it."

"I doubt it." Clar got up to walk to the fireplace and stood over it looking into the flames. Kennedy wanted to go to her and hold her, but was slightly afraid of her and what she could do.

"I won't hurt you. None of you. I would, however, like it if you would give me until sunrise before you kick me out." Kennedy snorted. As far as she was concerned, Clar was going nowhere. "You know as well as I do that he'll figure out where I am. There is no reason for you to harbor me in your home for any longer than necessary."

"'Tis my house and I will say who stays or goes." Clar looked at her, and Kennedy flushed. "I'm not ordering you about. I'm pissed at Stephen, if you need the truth of it."

"Me too." Kennedy might have laughed had the woman not looked so sad. "He only did what is in his nature. Feeding from me was what he does. Animals do what is in their nature."

Kennedy hurt for both of them. Stephen was a wonderful man, but whatever he'd done to Clar that had her thinking of him as an animal must have been very bad indeed. The marks on her throat were enough to tell her that he'd bitten her hard, and taken without any thought to what pain he might have caused her. She wondered briefly if he had raped her.

"It's none of your business. I know that you've given me shelter, and I appreciate it, but what happened at that house is no one's business but mine and his." Clar looked up from the fire at her. "Someone is coming. She is very upset."

Summer rolled into the room and stopped just short of them. She stared at Clar for a long time before she looked at Kennedy. The pain in her eyes was enough to make Kennedy go to her and see what hurt her. Summer Payne meant more to her than her own mother ever had.

"Stephen just called here. I won't tell you what he said to me, but suffice it to say, he is pissed off." Kennedy started to tell Summer it was all right when Clar took a step toward Summer.

"You hurt her and I will kill you." She had no idea why she'd suddenly got the feeling that Clar was going to do something to Summer, but she stood in front of her all the same. Summer touched her arm and asked her to move. Clar moved around her and knelt down to her level.

"Your spine was severed." Summer nodded. They stared at each other for long moments before Clar put her hand out and gently ran her finger down her arm, then back up. "I've all sorts of freaky skills right now. I can read minds and block assholes from mine. And he's trying very hard to get in. Then there is the added advantage that I can toss him back out with a little pain too."

"You should know that he will come here sooner rather than later." Summer touched Clar's face as she nodded. "He hurt you."

"As most people I know do. They learn what I have and take and take. And those that don't know just simply take." Kennedy watched the exchange between the two women and felt slightly jealous from it. When Clar looked at her, she thought she knew how she was feeling. Standing after a few seconds, Clar moved toward the door but stopped just short of going out. "He's on his way, so I'll take my leave. Mrs. Payne, I thank you for your hospitality. And Summer, you should really think about getting out of that chair."

Kennedy looked at her mother-in-law and could see the shock on her face. Turning to tell Clar that it was a cruel thing to say, she wasn't really surprised to find she was gone. Going to Summer, she knelt down much like Clar had.

"I'm so sorry she hurt ye." Summer shook her head. "She knew ye was hurt, and she said that to piss us off. I would imagine that she wants us to not follow—"

"I can feel my feet." Kennedy waited for her to say that she was kidding, but she nodded. "I can wiggle my toes too."

Kennedy tore off her mother-in-law's slippers, and they both watched as her toes did indeed wiggle. It was the most amazing sight she'd ever seen. When her foot suddenly stretched out in front of her, Kennedy stood up and helped her out of the chair. Summer staggered a little, but she eventually stood up on her own. Kennedy brushed at the tears that were streaming down her face.

"We must tell Samuel." Kennedy nodded and rushed out of the room, only to turn and help Summer back into her chair. "I'll just sit here and stand up when he comes in. Oh my, to stand again. Go and find the girl, too. I must...well I was going to say...go get Samuel."

Babbling. They were both babbling, and when she entered Samuel's office, she was sobbing so hard she could barely tell him what had happened. He came around his desk and to her just as the front door opened. There stood Stephen, and he did not look happy.

"Where is she?" Kennedy didn't care where the girl was and if she knew, she'd never tell him. She'd done this to Summer, she knew it, and as far as she was concerned, he could fuck off. "Clarice, where is she? I want her here right now."

"You want, you want...have you ever thought of what she might want?" He stretched his neck and glared. "Oh, ye think ye have a bit of temper, do you? Well, I'm an Irish woman who can turn into a lion and eat your temper for lunch. Sit down."

She was surprised when he sat. And she had to fight her laughter when he sat down on the floor. Moving past him, holding Samuel's hand, she took him to the study where his mom was.

"You just made him sit like a puppy. He's not going to be very happy with you when he realizes what you've done." She waved him off. "Mom, how are you?"

Samuel sat on the couch and looked at them both. She wasn't sure what to do and looked at Summer just as Stephen walked in. Pointing to the couch, she watched as he tried to stare her down. Eventually he sat down, but he didn't look happy about it.

"Clar was here, but she left when she...after she..." Kennedy smiled at Summer. "I think you should just show them."

They had moved the foot rests of the chair when she'd stood the first time, so they were out of the way. Summer gripped the handles as she shifted on the seat, and Samuel started to rise to no doubt help her. But Kennedy stopped him with a hand to his chest. It took Summer two tries, but she was standing on her own and looking at her son.

"Christ." Samuel did stand this time, and walked around his mom. She knew how he felt. It was just too much. "Clar did this?"

"Yes. Can you believe it? She just touched me." Summer sat back down, but not in the chair. She sat in one of the wingbacks near the fire as she continued. "She knew that my spine had been severed, and then she talked about how everyone uses her. And how she can block out assholes when necessary. Would that be you, Stephen?"

"She shouldn't be able to do that." Kennedy knew she shouldn't, but with the miracle that had happened just today, she wouldn't be surprised if the girl could do whatever the fuck she wanted. Summer looked at her before looking back at Stephen.

"I'm not going to help you find her. I have a connection to her because she healed me. I don't know where she is, but I can feel her." She lifted her arm and looked at it, and Kennedy did as well. The small mark there was where Clar had touched her. "It's fading. When I first saw it, the markings were dark; now they're just...they're fading. I would guess my connection to her will as well."

"She's turning you against me." Kennedy started to tell him to grow up, but Samuel hit him in the back of the head instead. "What the fuck was that for?"

"You're doing that all on your own, if you ask me. When I went to get her this morning, it was all I could do not to go up and stake you. What the fuck did you do to her anyway? And the blood. Christ, it looked like you tore at her throat."

Stephen got up to pace. Kennedy had never seen him this way, so upset and yet so broken looking. Samuel watched him as well, and she reached for her mate.

Did he rape her? He told her no. *But he did hurt her. Why, do you know? Why would a man, a mate, hurt his other half?*

Because I think it's more to do with the fact that he doesn't want her to get hurt more than he doesn't want her. He may not even realize how much he wants her in his life right now.

Kennedy was sure Samuel was right. When Stephen sat down again, he looked as if he'd come to a great decision. And whatever it was, he wasn't all that happy about it.

"She entered my mind when I was sleeping. I'm not sure why, but I doubt it was what I first thought. I think I might have accused her of spying on me." He stood up to pace. "She found something I've hidden so deep that I rarely think of it anymore...no, that's not true. I think of it all the time, but her knowing tore me up. I hurt her. I...I didn't mean to, but I did all the same."

"You bit her badly, Stephen. Her throat looked as if she'd been torn at. Did you do that to her?" He nodded at Summer. "And you took any trust, the very little that might have been there, away. She mentioned that she'd been used before. Do you think you did that to her?"

"I did." Summer nodded again as Stephen continued. "But now...Christ, now I have to have her. Not just because I want to keep her safe from everything else in my life, but because we've bonded and mated. She's mine. I'll never...what the hell am I supposed to do with her?"

"I would imagine that she can care for herself if you were to simply leave her alone as she's told you to do. As she has the rest of us as well." Stephen shook his head at Samuel. "I didn't say you should, I'm just telling you she looks to me like she can pretty much save her own ass if she needs to."

"A vampire is out for my ass. Her name is Velvet December. Or that's what she goes by now. We were lovers once, and she decided to throw me under the bus when she got caught at something. I turned her in, and she was sentenced to die. But they were more humane then and she wasn't killed. She's found out that I do business with Edward Barron, who just happens to be Clar's stepfather. I'm sure that neither of them know the connection yet, but they will sooner or later." Stephen sat down. "I've got a call into Barron now. I'm going to quit him as soon as possible, but I doubt it will do me much good. She's figured it out, and soon she'll find out about my mate."

"This Barron person, does he know that you are with Clar?" Stephen shrugged, then shook his head at her. Kennedy knew what he meant. He wasn't sure. "We'll have to find her, Clar I mean, before these people do."

"Yeah? You make it sound as if you might just pick up the phone and call her. I don't believe she'd answer even if she had a cell phone." They all looked up when Butler walked in the room. He looked confused.

"My lord, there is an officer at the door. He says that you are needed downtown. That he believes that your offices have been destroyed." Samuel stood up, but Butler shook his head. "I'm sorry, my lord, I meant Lord Silva."

~~~

Destroyed didn't even begin to cover the damage done to his offices. Stephen thought he'd be better off simply moving rather than trying to get someone to come in and repair this place. He picked up what was left of his computer and dropped it on the growing pile of things the police had asked him to go through. Why they needed to know if anything was missing was beyond him. Wasn't the damage here enough for them to go out and find out who did it?

"This December person, did she do this?" Stephen nodded at Samuel, who had come with him. "She's really pissed off at you."

"You think?" Stephen went to the large opening that had once held a window. Now it was letting in the cold air. Looking down at the lot below, he could see that someone had thrown his desk down there to no doubt bust the glass. "She wasn't alone. Another vampire was with her, and he did most of the heavier work. But the blood here is a human."

She'd written him a message in human blood. And from the looks of it, it might have killed the person too. Stephen looked at the message again.

I found you. And now that I have, I will stop at nothing to get you back between my legs, fucking me for all of eternity.

"She's very poetic." Stephen looked at the man speaking and nodded. The police officer had been the one who had met him downstairs when they'd arrived. "I don't suppose you will tell me who she is? And why she is so pissed at you? Did you leave her hanging?"

The man was kidding, of course, but Stephen felt his beast rise. The smell of blood notwithstanding, he was pissed too. Walking away, he let Samuel deal with the officer. He went to the bathroom that had curiously not been touched, walked in, and shut the door. Reaching again for Clar, he nearly cried out when he was able to contact her.

You should know that someone is hanging around my stepfather's house that knows you. She and he are having a wonderful time of it, I think. He could hear her sarcasm. Before he could ask her if she was all right, she continued. *When she first arrived, he had locked her out, but that did him little good. She just busted in the door and screamed at him. After a bit, she got in. I'm guessing she had to be invited.*

She did. She's looking for me, I would imagine. You're not safe there, or anywhere, for that matter. You should go back to my house.

No. I'm only allowing you to contact me because I think you should know that this woman is going to use Edward to kill you. Not that I really give a shit what happens to you, but I like Summer, and she loves you. He didn't ask her how she knew that, but she continued anyway, and he never got the chance. *I came by the house to see if I could get some cash. I'm going to be leaving the area soon, so you don't have to worry about us accidently bumping into each other again.*

I'm sorry. He started to say more, but she cut him off. Stephen knew that for as long as he lived, he'd never forgive himself for hurting her the way that he had.

Fuck off. You got what you wanted, so why the hell should I care if you're sorry or not? Anyway, it doesn't matter really. I'm going to be gone and you'll be the same fucking dick shit that you've always been. He heard her anger but knew that letting his own temper get the better of him wasn't going to help. *There is a man going in the house now. He's like you, a vampire. Wait.*

Stephen did wait but not by standing idle until she got back to him. He moved out of the bathroom and into the offices to Samuel. He was going to see if he could find her and bring her to safety. After telling Samuel where he was headed, he left the building and willed himself to the address. He had no idea where she was, but he could smell the other vampires nearby.

"You were told to wait." Her voice behind him startled him. Turning toward her, he looked at what he'd done to her.

"I did hurt you." She jerked away from his touch when he made to pull her to him. "I'm so sorry. I was...it matters little what I was feeling. I should never have taken it out on you."

"I'm used to it." Stephen felt the stab of her words in his heart. He had no use for a mate, but she was his, and he had hurt her in ways that tore at him. Before he could try to even make it up to her, she started talking again. "They're moving. I'm not sure where to, but the female took Edward away about a minute ago, and the other vamp is moving through the house like he's on a mission."

"They're probably looking for money or something valuable to sell." He closed his eyes and reached into the house. That's what the man was doing, and when he turned so that Stephen could get a look at his face, he realized he knew him. "His name is Ted. I'm not sure if I ever learned his last name or not, but he is her day walker. Or he used to be. She must have converted him sometime over the past few days."

"When he leaves, you should follow him." Stephen didn't bother telling her that wasn't going to happen. When she left, he was going to go too. "The house has a safe, and it's doubtful that even Edward knew about it. My mom…she set it up for us. In the event something happened to her."

"Did he kill her?" Clarice moved away from him without answering, and Stephen thought he knew. She made her way to the house, and Stephen knew as surely as she did that Ted had left. She moved into the house while he stood at the door. "You have to invite me in."

He hadn't expected her to and wasn't surprised when she kept moving deeper in the house. Stephen waited by the door hoping that she came this way and not out some hidden passage while he stood there. It would be just what he deserved if she left him there for the sun to take.

When she appeared twenty minutes later, he watched her stuff something into a bulging pack. He also noticed that she had a laptop bag, as well as a nice-sized jewelry box. He reached for some of the things when she was standing in front of him. Again he wasn't surprised when she didn't let him carry them.

"I've enough here to live on for a while." He didn't answer her because there wasn't any way he was going to agree to her leaving him. "Here. These belong to you."

The envelope was heavy, and he glanced inside before looking up at her again. They were the missing recordings from his office, he'd bet, something that he'd never told anyone about. He would bet any amount of money that Ted had taken them because Velvet wouldn't have known about such things.

"Will you come back to my home with me? I would like to talk to you." She shook her head. "Please? I know that I've given you no reason to trust me, but I'd like to—"

"You're right, I have no reason to trust you. And it's very doubtful even if you were to tell me why you are no different than Edward is that I'd believe you." She looked away but not before he saw the tears. "Men like you deserve whatever happens to you. I've never hurt anyone in my life. But I've been abused more than…yes, he killed my mother. Hired a man to rob the car we were in, but he got greedy and killed her. Then he…I don't know if Edward was there, but someone hit me when he saw that I was watching him from the side seat. Hit me with the ball bat that had been used to kill my mother. And as I lay there dying, watching the two people I could no longer see take her jewelry off her hands and wrists, one of them spit on me."

"But you didn't die and were enhanced somehow. Do you know why?" She shook her head, and he raised his hand to touch her face. When she backed away, he held his ground until she nodded once. "I'm going to only look at what happened."

The pain hit him first. He had no idea that a human could endure so much. But then he realized it wasn't from the wound but from what he'd done to her. Moving deeper into her mind, he touched the area of her mind that held so much magic that he was amazed by it. And there he saw what he needed. Pulling back from her, he stared at her for several seconds before he spoke.

"The faeries healed you. Their magic is why you lived when you should have died." She didn't say anything, and Stephen figured she knew it. "My blood gave you the rest. Enough to heal Summer for us."

This time when she moved past him, he let her. Stephen moved to follow, and she didn't stop him. They were nearly to the gate again when someone pulled into the drive. He pulled her back just as the car turned toward them. They watched as a large van drove by them. Looking down at her, he could see that she was out. Touching her head gently, he saw that he'd knocked her onto a rock and he'd rendered her unconscious. Stephen picked her up and wondered if there would ever be a time when he didn't hurt her somehow. He took them back to his home.

Chapter 7

Edward sat as still as he could so that they'd not notice him. He was terrified beyond reason right now and didn't want to spook the woman into a rage again. She'd been so violent that his arm had been broken and his head had been knocked against the wall hard enough to knock him out. When he'd awakened ten minutes ago tied to a chair, he found he was in her house and not his, and that his body was healed again.

"You think that I don't know what you're thinking?" He wasn't sure if she was talking to him or the other man next to him. He was dead, of course. She'd killed him as soon as Edward had woke, but he wouldn't put it past her to talk to the dead. "I'm speaking to you, Eddie. Do you think I can't read your mind?"

"I don't know. Can you?" The pain behind his eyes was incredible, and he cried out with it. She laughed at him.

"I can do just about anything I want to you and you'll love it. Won't you?" She was suddenly naked, and Edward felt his cock jerk. She had some sort of sexual power over him, and he hated her for it. "You're going to fuck me again."

"No, please no." She moved toward him, nodding. "I'm not in the mood. I don't want to hurt again."

"You'll be in the mood for me. Let me show you." His clothes were suddenly gone, and he looked down at his erection. Christ, he was bruised and cut and wondered what the hell they'd done to him. But she dropped to her knees in front of him and wrapped her hand around his thickening cock. He moaned when she licked his crown.

"Don't." But it was too late. She sucked his cock, bringing him close to the edge twice before she stood up. He leaned back in the chair to allow her to sit over him and felt his cock being swallowed by her pussy.

"You're so good at fucking me." He moaned again when she started riding him. He realized suddenly his hands were free, and he lifted her breast to his mouth while he held her hips. "Bite me, Eddie. Bite me hard and suck the blood out of my tit."

He did as she commanded him to do and he tasted her blood. The taste had him coming hard, and he slid his finger in her ass when she told him to. Lifting his head up by his hair, she showed him her fangs. Nothing in the world could have stopped him from tilting his head to give her his throat.

The bite was painful, but as soon as she sucked at him, he felt his balls tighten to his body. His climax was close again. Grabbing both her hips, he lifted her up and took her to the desk and spread her over it. He pounded in her hard enough to have her scooting away from him. Holding her by the shoulders while she fed from him, he nearly cried out when someone touched his ass. Knowing who it was without looking, he welcomed Ted into his ass.

The pain was bliss, and he came screaming out both their names as he emptied himself in Velvet. He felt Ted bite him hard at the shoulder as the man came in him and felt his cock let go again. Edward came an incredible third time when Velvet tightened around his cock again. He was light headed when she pulled away from his throat.

Edward wasn't sure how he made it to the couch, but he was suddenly sitting there watching as Ted fucked Velvet in the ass. Her breasts bounced in time to his taking her, and Edward reached down to fist his cock. When Ted cried out he was coming, Edward did as well, spraying his cum all over his body and the pillow next to him. He watched as the two of them kissed. If someone would have tried to attack him right now, he knew that he'd simply let them. He was completely drained sexually and anything else they'd done to him.

"You have cum on your face." Edward reached up and wiped his face with his hand and grimaced when it came away with cum on it. He looked at Velvet to see her smiling at him. "Are you going to piss me off again by leaving us?"

Edward looked at Ted, who was lounging in the chair across from him stroking his cock. He'd done it again…Edward had let a man fuck him. Looking at Velvet, he shivered. He was afraid that if he tried to leave again, she'd kill him.

"And you'd be right." She picked up his hand and laid it over her breast. Her nipple hardened under his touch, and she pulled him toward her. Taking her breast into his mouth, he felt his cock harden again, but she pulled him back before he could get fully hard. "I asked you a question."

"You know I can't. And as much as I hate myself afterwards, the sex is incredible." He looked at Ted when he laughed. "Why do you fuck me when you know how much I hate it?"

"I doubt you hate it as much as you say. You come pretty hard for a man who hates me sucking him off and fucking his pretty ass, too." Edward wanted to deny it, but Ted cut him off. "If I were to come to you right now and take your cock in my mouth, you'd squirt down my throat faster than I could swallow, and we both know it."

To no doubt prove his point, he stood up and sat down in front of Edward. Before he could get away, if that was even what he wanted, Ted was sucking his cock hard enough to have him cry out. Edward curled his fingers in Ted's hair while Velvet moved to put her pussy over his mouth. He ate her as his cock was being fisted, deep in another man's throat. When she came, screaming out his name, Edward emptied his cock in Ted's mouth.

"My turn." Ted leaned back, and he held his cock while Velvet moved over him. It was the most erotic thing he'd ever witnessed, and when she told him to come to her, he stood in front of her. She took him in her mouth even as she rolled her hips over Ted's cock. When a finger filled his ass, Edward fucked her mouth hard. Christ, nothing had ever felt this good. When Ted cupped his balls from beneath, Edward held Velvet to his cock while he came again. The three of them came at nearly the same time, and Edward wanted to cry.

Staggering back, he fell into the chair that Ted had been in. Velvet lay over Ted, and the man ran his finger up and down her back while he stared at him. He wanted to tell him to go to hell, but the smile he was giving Edward sort of frightened him.

"She wants to change you." Edward started to ask him into what, but he suddenly knew. "I'm having her wait for a while. You will be more useful to us if you can be out during the day. Are you going to prove me wrong?"

"I don't want to be a vampire." He felt his skin crawl. He knew he was fucking two of them and had them biting him like he was some sort of all-day sucker for them, but he didn't want to live as one. Not ever. "I'll do whatever you want during the day, but I don't want to be a vampire."

"We'll see." He stood up then after rolling Velvet to the floor. Leaning down, he picked her up as if she weighed nothing at all and looked at him. "Your house will be gone by now. And I'd stay away from the windows if I were you too. You've had enough of our blood in you that you're likely to burn a good deal. And without us here to give you more, you'll hurt until we wake."

After he left him, the same butler from before came in with a tray of food. There was also an envelope on the tray. Edward didn't even bother asking but waited until he was gone before he opened it. He was shoveling his breakfast down as fast as he could put it on his fork while he read it.

I want you to have a meeting with Stephen tonight. I need to kill him before he realizes that you and I are lovers. He shivered at the thought but continued reading. *If you leave this house without my permission, I will kill you. And when I do, it will be long and painful for you. Do as I said.*

He felt his breakfast curl in his belly as he moved away from it. There wasn't much of it left, but he was sure he'd not be able to eat any more now. Going to the window, he looked out over the yards and saw that the entire estate was now surrounded by a high fence. Even if he wanted to, Edward was sure that he wouldn't be able to get out so easily again. Moving out of the room, he went in search of the kitchen again and found the butler there.

"I need a phone and a computer if you have one." He nodded and stood up. Edward sat down when the woman that had been there too sat a glass in front of him. He toyed with it while he waited for the butler to return. The computer was set on the table, as was a cell phone. Looking at the man who sat again, he wondered how much he knew about why he was there.

"I have taken the liberty of having all your calls transferred to this number. The lady of the house would not like for you to miss important things, and she would be furious with us if someone came here to find you. Do not tell them where we are." Edward nodded and stared at the phone as the man continued. "You would do well to do as she said, sir. If not, there will be hell to pay."

"Does she do this often?" The man looked at the woman, who nodded and left them alone. He nearly told the man to forget it, he didn't want to know, when he spoke.

"She has only just risen again, my lord. We have been…until a month ago, we were far away, hiding. The lady said we were hers and there was little we could do. We had been her servants before she was…sentenced."

"Sentenced?" He nodded, and Edward didn't ask. There were some things he knew he just shouldn't know. "I don't want to be here. What we do…they're making me do, is not something I want."

"You will serve their purpose or you will die." Edward knew in his heart that he was right and nodded. "Many have come before you, but none have stayed in her graces as you have. You must please her greatly."

Edward stood up. He hadn't wanted this but knew that it was too late now for anything to be done about it. He wondered if they'd changed him anyway, and if there was a damned thing he could do to stop this madness. He was nearly to the office again when the phone in his hand rang. He nearly didn't answer it but in the end did.

"I found her." It took him several seconds to realize that this was Hump-boy. "Your daughter. I found her. And you're not going to believe where. With none other than your biggest client, Stephen Silva."

"She's with Silva? Since when? And what the hell would he be doing with a dog like her?" He heard Hump laugh. "You find this humorous? Need I remind you that I still haven't paid you, and won't until she's back with me in my home?"

"Yeah, about that. Your house went up in a blaze of fire late last night. They're saying it was set, but nobody is saying by who. And there is so little of it left that they're having a grand old time trying to figure out what was used to blow it, much less by who." Edward sat down, just now remembering what Ted had told him before leaving. "But as I was watching the fire stations sort through things, Silva drives up, and with him is this drop-dead gorgeous woman. It took me nearly an hour to get her name. It's Clarice Kelley. And she doesn't look any more thrilled to be with him than she apparently did with you."

"Gorgeous? Her? Hardly. She was a grown woman when she left, and it's doubtful that she's made that much of a change. I'm assuming you've mistaken her for someone else. Silva would never have someone like that, for that matter, especially a fat tub like her hanging around him." Edward decided to get rid of Hump and find someone more reliable. But then his phone beeped at him, and he looked at it. A message had come through. Opening it up, he looked at the picture that had come from Hump. It was her.

She was considerably thinner...he'd say a whole person thinner, and she looked as if she'd not only slimmed down but had become toned. The picture cut off her legs, but Edward knew that they'd be long and slim too. Her hair was still long, but it flattered her face rather than looking like it hung in front of it. Edward realized that Hump was talking to him and put the phone to his ear again.

"It's her, right? I knew it. Damn, but she's really done herself up right. And poor Silva looks like he'd do just about anything for her, but she barely lets him touch her. I think the only reason she was even with him is because she seemed to have gotten out of his bed or something. She had on his shirt and a pair of baggy jeans. Didn't hide the fact that she was beautiful, but made her look sexier somehow."

Edward wanted to scream at Hump to shut up, but didn't want him to know how much his words were affecting him. Edward did not want to know that the product was doing better than he was, and was a good deal richer to boot. He told Hump he'd talk to him later and hung up. Maybe he'd just call Silva up and have him give him Kelley for the knowledge that a crazy woman was gunning for him. He knew that he'd have liked that information a few weeks ago.

He picked up the phone twice to do just that. But Edward was worried that it wouldn't work, or if it did and Silva was killed, Velvet would know he'd done it. Right now he was more afraid of her than the big man and losing his money. Finally he called Silva to test the waters, so to speak, and was surprisingly put right through to him.

"Stephen, how the hell are you? I've been thinking of that last job we did for you and wondered if you were still having good luck with it." Edward had no idea what they'd worked on for him and was pretty sure that the man knew it too. But when he didn't say anything, Edward began to worry. "Stephen, are you there?"

"I am. How did Velvet find you?" He felt the hair on the back of his neck dance and his balls tighten to his body in a defense mode. "I'm assuming that's why you're calling me, to see if we can make some sort of deal on turning her over to me. Or is it because of Clarice? Are you still looking for her for some perverted reason?"

"I don't know what you're ref—" Silva's laughter cut him off. All he could think about was he was as good as dead, and there wasn't shit he could do about it. "She came to me. And she knew all about you and I having dealings. I didn't know what she was until recently. She made me do things that were not something I would ever do."

"But you no doubt enjoyed them. Is Ted with her still? I had heard that he'd been changed as well. I'm supposing you know that I'm a vampire as well." Edward felt his body turn to ice. He'd been told he'd been dealing with a vampire all this time and not had a clue, but to have the man say it was something else entirely. More real, he supposed. "You should also understand that not only am I a good deal older than her, I'm also not one you want to fuck with. I could eat you for breakfast and not think a thing about it. I just might before this is over. *If* you survive Velvet December."

"Are you going to kill me?" His laughter again made Edward reach down and curl his hand over his cock. Not because he was hard but because he was worried he'd wet himself. "I don't want to die."

"I'm reasonably sure it's too late for that. You've been with two of the deadliest vampires in the world right now. The fact that you're still living is somewhat of a miracle. Are they still as sick in bed as they've always been? Have you told her about Clarice yet?"

He told him no. "But she knows everything. It's like she can read my mind." Edward was trying to think of a way to escape, but all he could think about was that Stephen was truly a vampire too. "She's very violent when she's pissed off."

"Not nearly so much as I am. And you're right, she'll figure out you know about my mate. I guess you'll have to deal with her when she does. Unless, of course, you expect me to help you. If you do, you're stupider than I ever thought you were." Edward didn't want to deal with anyone, especially not a pissed off vampire. "You might want to find a gun."

"I doubt she'd let me shoot her." Silva laughed, and this time it pissed Edward off more than scared him. "This is not the least bit funny. You people should tell someone when you're not human so we can avoid you."

"Maybe we don't think it's any of your business." He heard someone talking in the background and wondered who he was. Stephen spoke again before Edward could make it out. "By the way, shit for brains, the gun isn't for you to shoot her with, you moron, but to shoot yourself. It might be a good deal quicker than what I have planned for you. Or Velvet for that matter. I'm thinking you might want me over her in the long run."

The line went dead, and Edward laid the phone down. He was more terrified now than he'd ever been. Searching though the drawers, he didn't find as much as a paperclip to end his life, or at least end it quicker. He was still sitting there when the butler brought him his lunch. And Edward's only thought that kept curling around and around in his brain was that he wanted Stephen to kill him over the bitch that slept below.

"What am I going to do?" The butler didn't answer, but then he'd not really expected him to. "I have to save my ass here. If I could get out to...fuck I don't know, bring Silva here, then she'd be okay, right?"

Nothing. But the idea was starting to take shape. Not with Silva. The man scared the shit out of him even before he'd found out what he was. No, he was thinking more along the lines of getting Kelley, the bitch. If he could get her, bring her here, then that would bring Silva to Velvet. It would work. But first he had to get out. He finished what he could of his lunch and planned.

The doors out of the house were all locked up. When he moved to the doors that led out onto the back deck, he wasn't really surprised to find them locked as well. But the windows were just plain glass, and he seriously thought about breaking them. Just as he was picking up a chair to bash it through the thing, the butler came back in.

"Sir, there is someone here to see you." Edward started to back away even before the man continued. "He said he is with the insurance company that holds the policy on your home, and spoke with you earlier. Where would you like for me to set him up?"

"I don't know, in here?" The man started out but turned back to him. He looked at the glass doors and then at the chair. Edward knew he had figured it out.

"If you were to tell the man what is going on in this household, sir, she will kill you. Not easily, I would imagine. If I were you, I would only answer what he asks of you, and perhaps bring up your plan with the mistress when she next rises. It might...you may live a good deal longer." Edward nodded. "Very good, sir. I'll bring in coffee, shall I?"

After he left with the trolley of his lunch plates, Edward sat down. It wasn't a threat. It was a way for him to get by without being killed. He wondered why the man had done it, but didn't care. Edward would do just what the butler had said and then figure out a way to tell Velvet his plan without making himself look desperate. He had no idea if he could pull it off, but it was his only hope.

As soon as Cantor Shill came into the room, Edward felt the need to tell him everything, but all he did was sit down and go over the papers. It seemed that the house fire was under investigation, and it would be a while before he was paid.

"I understand. I don't know what happened, as I've been staying with my friends for a few days, but—"

"A weight loss guru, right?" Edward looked at him. He was confused by the question. "You look like you've dropped about eighty pounds. I don't know what this guy is doing for you, but you're looking a little...well, I'd not lose much more if I were you. You're going to get ill. I mean, you needed to lose the weight but, damn, you are too thin if you ask me."

"I've been...I'm working on getting in better shape." Edward felt a burble of laughter catch in his throat. Yeah, he thought to himself, I'm working on getting dead is what I'm doing. He wanted to tell the adjustor that being butt fucked by an Amazon while sucking off some vampire's pussy was an amazing weight loss program, if you could stand to have them biting you and drinking you dry on a daily basis.

Edward was making notes after Shill left. The money mattered little to him at the moment. In fact, he figured he had a good deal stashed away if he wanted to simply build again. But he was more concerned with living until tomorrow. He was going over his notes when Velvet came into the room. For once she was alone.

"I've got an idea." She sat down across from him and stared at him. He'd seen this look before on her. It said she was going to hurt him if he didn't get to the point. "I can have Silva come here, but I need to go and get his mate first."

"Mate? Silva has a mate?" She perked up, and Edward had a moment to wonder if he'd been wrong about this mate business and it wasn't just some fuck buddy he'd found. "That's rich. He didn't smell like he'd found any female when I was at his place of business. This is great. What do you need?"

"His mate is my stepdaughter. If I could go and get her, bring her here, I think he'd come here to get her." Velvet started nodding even before he finished. "She doesn't like me overly much, but that won't be a problem if I can kidnap her. She owes me anyway."

"You'll take a few wolves I know. They'll know that you're in charge, and if need be, they'll simply tear her up a little to make her easier to subdue." Edward liked the idea. He thought he'd pay real money to see Kelley eaten by a pack of wolves. "When do you want to do this? I'd like to be around, but I know that she's more than likely human, so you'll need to take her during the day."

They planned for another hour before she stripped down to her bare skin and crawled up on his lap just as Ted came into the room. As much as he hated what was going to happen next, he hated it more that his cock was hard as stone, and his mouth was watering for another taste of either of them. Edward would gladly have put a gun to his head at that moment.

STEPHEN

Chapter 8

Stephen was sick of walking around as if the house where a bomb and the slightest sound would make it go off. He moved into the kitchen to see if he could find Clarice, but all that was in the room was Kasen. He didn't look any happier than Stephen felt.

"She is out of doors with Master Vinnie. They have been out there for over an hour." Stephen started to the door, only to stop when Kasen said his name. "Sire, may I be so bold as to ask you what you are going to do once you go out there?"

"I suppose whatever I was planning will piss you and her off, so why don't you tell me what I should do?" He hated himself as soon as the words left his mouth. "I'm sorry. I've been a real bastard for the past several days and I don't know what to do about it."

"I'm sure you do." Stephen waited for him to say more, and when he didn't immediately, he looked out the door to see that Vinnie was talking to her and pointing to the trees. He looked up and saw a beautiful hawk there and wondered if it was their friend, Hawk. When the bird came down and landed on Vinnie's arm, he figured it wasn't.

Hawk was a great man, but he didn't do tricks. When Kasen cleared his throat, Stephen spoke first.

"She hates me, you know. I'm not sure if it's because I'm a vampire, or simply because of who I am. Not that I blame her. I've not been the most friendly guy before she came along, and I've not changed all that much since she's been here." Stephen watched her back away from Vinnie when he seemed to get a little too close, if you could call five or six feet too close. "I guess I should be happy I'm not the only one she's afraid of."

"She's not afraid of you, my lord, but I do believe she is afraid." He looked at Kasen. "Watch her. The faeries that are there are not touching her either. It is as if they too can sense that she is a bit..."

"Standoffish?" Kasen shook his head and watched her for a few more minutes with him. She did seem to avoid touch, completely. When Leith landed on her shoulder, Clarice picked her up and set her on a nearby bush. "Why is she like that?"

"I have heard from Master Samuel that she has lived alone for a number of years. And before that, her stepfather had been abusive toward her." Stephen nodded but watched Clarice as she backed away from Vinnie when he shifted again. "Perhaps she has forgotten how to let anyone close to her; mayhap she is...sire, I do believe the girl is lonely."

He looked at his long-time day walker and thought he was kidding. There had been any number of people in and out of his house since he'd brought her there, and most of them looked at him as if he were carrying a disease or something. Even Kennedy had been a little short with him. Of course, that could have been because he'd growled at her for being there in the first place. Stephen looked back at Clarice and thought of what Kasen had said.

Lonely. Okay, if you were afraid of someone finding you all the time, he knew that you'd sort of become a recluse. Even a hermit, maybe. He'd been one until recently, and still caught himself hiding away in his home rather than be around people. She'd been in a cave for the better part of a year too, with no friends, and as far as he could tell, no job either. He knew that she'd been in the diner, but then she'd not sat at the bar but at a table close to the door to make a quick escape. Stephen thought Kasen could be onto something.

"What do I do?" Kasen laughed a little and Stephen turned to look at him. "She's my mate and I have no idea what to do with her. She's...I want her. More than I have ever wanted a woman before, but she keeps..."

He wasn't going to tell his manservant that his mate wouldn't have sex with him. There were just some things that he had to keep to himself. But even though he kept his mouth shut, Stephen knew that Kasen knew everything.

"You should take her out. To dinner." He looked at him again. "You do not have to have a meal, sire, but you could take her out. Maybe for a pizza or even to a burger place. I know that she enjoys them. She requested I purchase the items to make them just yesterday. And I have refused her money, before you ask me."

"She tried to buy her own food?" Kasen nodded. "I can afford to buy her whatever she wants. I've more money than...Christ, I have more money than I know what to do with."

"Yet she wears your castoffs." Stephen looked at her shirt and pants. The shirt she had on he thought had been tossed to the rag pile some months ago. And the pants...well, he was sure he'd never owned them. He only ever wore dress pants and silk shirts. A suit and tie was his natural state of dress whenever he left the house, and sometimes when he was working from home. Looking at Kasen again, Stephen realized that he was dressed better than his mate. And he'd only just realized she was not wearing a coat either.

"Could you call Kennedy and Gab for me? And Thor too. I'm not sure she knows all that much about fashion, but she might know something." Kasen nodded and asked when. "I guess tomorrow."

"Perhaps it would be best if you talked it over with her ladyship and see when would be good for her." Stephen nodded. Yeah, that was another thing she'd argued with him about. He was forever bossing her around. "I will make the calls, sire, when you have spoken to her ladyship."

"Good." Stephen started out the door again and looked back. "You've probably saved me from making an ass of myself."

"It's what I live for, sire. And you've been doing such a good job of it lately that I thought you'd need a break." Stephen was out the door when it occurred to him that he'd just been insulted. But instead of being pissed about it, he laughed. Kasen was a good deal slicker than he'd ever thought him to be.

Clarice turned to look at him when he was nearly to her. Stephen looked at her in a different light now. She wasn't just getting away from him, he thought, but people in general. Vinnie pulled him in for a big hug, which he returned. They had been friends for a very long time.

"I thought you were with Hawk." Vinnie laughed and shook his head at his statement. "The pretty hawk there, do you know if she has a nest about or at least close by?"

"Close, and yes, a nest. Hawk and I have been helping her out. Her mate was killed a few weeks ago, and she had four chicks." Stephen noticed that Clarice moved away from him when he took a step toward her. He wanted to tell her he'd never harm her, but knew that it would just piss her off again. Instead he ran his finger down her arm before moving away again. He'd show her in small doses if he had to. "Did Vinnie tell you he is a dragon?"

"He did. He said someday he'd give me a ride." She lifted her chin as she glared at him. "He said I'd need your permission first, and I told him you didn't own me."

"I don't. I would ask that you let me know if you go on a ride, but you can go when you want." She looked confused, and he didn't blame her. It was a lot easier than he'd thought it would be to not be a bastard. He just hoped he could keep it up for her. "I'd like to talk to you about something later if you don't mind?"

"Tell me something or talk *at* me?" Vinnie laughed, and she flushed. "I'm sorry. That was rude of me in front of your friend."

"So, it's okay if you're rude to me in private?" He smiled to try and take the bite out of what he'd said. "I think we've both been rude to each other, and I'm mostly to blame."

"I'm not going to disagree with you, but I should just learn to keep my mouth shut." Vinnie laughed again. Clarice looked at him. "When you find your mate, will you treat her as an object as he does, or will you give her as much compassion as you do your animals?"

"I'm not going to find my mate. Even if she's out there, which I'm not saying she is, but I think she'd take one look at me and my beast and run for the hills. I certainly would." Clarice looked at him, then at Vinnie again. He could tell what she was thinking. That they were alike. The difference was, he'd found his mate and she hated him. Vinnie's was still to come.

After another ten minutes or so, Vinnie's phone went off and he said he had to go. There was a project that was giving him fits and he was trying to work it out. After he left, Clarice started for the house and he stopped her.

"Do you have a coat you can put on?" She shook her head, and he took off his jacket. "I don't really need it, but I'd like to show you something on the other end of the property. It's not far, but it's cold."

"I don't want your coat." She shivered as he moved behind her to help her slip it on. "I'm just fine the way I am."

"Please?" She let him put it on her, and when he pulled her hair out of the coat, he lifted it to his nose. "You smell of my shampoo. I'm sorry for that. I should have had Kasen get you something more girly."

"There is no reason for you to go to the extra expense. If you'd rather I didn't use your things, just say so and I can use soap. I have before." He took her hand and held it until she stopped trying to pull away. "Do you always get what you want?"

"Yes." He held her hand as they moved toward the tree line. "Most people are afraid of me. I'm not a mean man, but I guess I'm a tad on the intense side. As for the shampoo, I didn't mean I didn't want you to use mine, but I thought you'd like something of your own."

"I can get my own things if I do." He nodded and waited for her to speak again. He was really trying to figure out a way to bring up her wardrobe, and when she spoke, he almost missed what she said. "Mr. Kasen said he'd do my laundry. I have a few extra clothes and thought I could just wash them up, but he insisted."

"I'm glad you brought that up. I was wondering if you'd allow me to get you some things to wear." She jerked at her hand, and he stopped and looked at her rather than let her go. "I assure you that I can afford it. And I really want to buy them for you. I've been remiss in not taking care of it before now. You need so many things."

"You think I'm poor? Do you think that if you buy me a few dresses that I'll let you fuck me again?" He felt his temper rise and tried his best to rein it in. "I'm not a cheap whore that you can buy off with pretty things."

"No, you're not. You're my mate." He pulled her body to his, and he felt his beast rise. "You're driving me insane with need. Do you know that? I want to press you to the closest tree and take you hard and fast. Then when I've satisfied just a little of the craving I have for you, I want to take you to my lair and make love to you over and over until you're as sated as I am."

Stephen pulled her up by her ass, and she wrapped her legs around his waist. He wanted to make her want him, delve into her mind and show her what it could be like if she'd only let him. When she wrapped her arms around his shoulders, he moaned and took her mouth. Christ, she tasted better than he remembered.

The tree seemed miles away, but he moved them toward it. As soon as he had her pressed against it, he lifted her higher until her breasts were at his mouth. Suckling at them through her shirt, he knew immediately that she was braless and lifted his head from her bounty.

"Feed me." She reached down with trembling fingers and pulled one of the buttons free before she looked up at him. He could see her lust. Her need was as hard as his.

"Tell me now that you don't want me. If you don't, then I'm going to take you now."

"It changes nothing." He growled low and watched her fingers work at the next button. "I don't love you. I'm not...I'm not capable of it."

He put his hands on the hem of the shirt and ripped it open. Her breasts were tight with her need, and her nipples were hard as his cock. Licking first one then the other, he looked at her again.

"This changes everything, and you know it. And though I don't love you either, we'll see what tomorrow brings us." He took her mouth again before she could speak. Then moving down her neck to her breast again, he suckled hard enough at her nipple to have her cry out. He rocked hard against her pussy as he slid his hands down the back of her pants. The tearing sound echoed through the woods.

"Not here." Stephen growled again at her. "Please, there are others here. Many of them, and I don't want them watching us."

Nodding, he held her to him and willed them to his lair. He'd never had a woman in there before, and promised himself he'd show her around later; but right now, he wanted to be buried as deep in her as he could get and empty himself in her.

~~~

Clar was nervous. Now that he'd done as she'd asked, she wasn't sure what do to. Their sex before...it had been so consuming that she was overwhelmed by it and him. She pushed at his shoulders when he laid her on the bed.

"Should we be using condoms?" He smiled at her, and she felt stupid. "I'm not ready for kids yet, and I don't know you well enough to know if you're full of something I don't want to catch. You've probably been with hundreds of women."

"Probably." She slapped his chest and noticed that he was bare. Running her fingers over his bare chest, she touched his nipple and felt it pucker under her fingers. "Don't stop touching me, please. I'm as sensitive as you are there."

"I've never touched a man before." When he didn't tell her to stop, she moved her hand to his other breast. "When I was in high school, I was fat. And the only guy who would have sex with me wasn't into foreplay."

"You really shouldn't talk about other men in our bed." He moaned when she rolled his nipple between her thumb and finger. "You want to explore me? I'll allow it, but you will return the favor."

"Explore you how?" He rolled to his back, taking her with him. He was naked, she realized, and sat up, feeling his cock at her ass. "Have you had sex with a great many women?"

She ran her fingers over his chest to his navel and smiled when he sucked in his belly. His groan had her pulling away from him, but he put her hands back. Clar looked at him.

"You may touch me anywhere you wish. I will tell you that I like what you're doing and what I don't like if you will tell me as well." She nodded. "Now where were we? Oh yes, women. Yes, a great many. Men too if you want to know. But I've been around a very long time. Almost three thousand years. Sex had become…well, boring I guess you could say. I played where I wanted and with whom I wanted. But as for diseases, I can't get them or give them to you, or anyone for that matter."

Her fingers danced along his ribs and he moaned. She found she liked the sound and looked for other places to touch him to hear it. When he put his hands on her hips, she thought he was going to pull her off him, but all he did was adjust her. She felt his cock now as it pressed between her nether lips. It was the most erotic thing she'd ever felt.

"You're wet." She nodded and moaned when he rolled his hips upward. "Have you ever masturbated?"

"Yes. It's not all that satisfying. But then sex in general isn't." She rolled her hips when he did and moaned again. "Except with you. I come a great deal with you."

"As do I with you." This time when he gripped her hips, he told her to sit up on her knees. "I'm going to show you how to ride me. I know you wish to explore, but I need to be inside of you now."

He held his cock as he helped her lower herself over him. He filled her, completely. And when she sat back on him, he was deeper still. As he pulled her hips forward, she realized what he wanted.

Touching him, she knew, brought him pleasure, but she was enjoying it too. Maybe more than him. When he held her hips, she again thought he was going to stop her, but he only held her to him. When he took her hands and put them to her breasts, the weight of them in her hands made her want to touch every part of herself as well.

"Lift them up and play with your nipples." She did as he instructed and cried out when he sat up. His groin touched her clit, and she thought she'd come just from that. "Do you have any idea how beautiful you are right now? Riding me and giving yourself pleasure is a sight I'll never forget."

"I want you to suck my nipples." He didn't hesitate but lifted one up with her hands and suckled at just the tip. "Harder please? I could come this way."

He nipped at her, and she cried out. The next time he bit her, she came apart with a quick but satisfying climax. She started to roll off him when he held her again.

"Not yet. I need you to let me feed from you." She looked at him, not really understanding until he showed her his fangs. "I won't hurt you, but I'd very much like to nurse from your breast and take my fill of you."

She rocked forward hard, wondering if he was serious. Her pussy heated up just watching him lick the tip of her breast, and then she held onto him when he took more of her into his mouth. The tiny pinch was gone almost as soon as she felt it, but then he suckled hard and she cried out. She felt his bite through her entire body.

"More." He groaned when she begged him for more. "Please, I need more. I want to come with you. Please, Stephen, help me."

He rolled her over until her back was on the bed. She wrapped her ankles around him as he moved in and out of her. Stephen lifted his head and looked at her and she saw blood, her blood, on his mouth.

"When I come in you, I want you to feed from me." She nodded, then shook her head. "You don't wish to find the same pleasure I do when I feed from you?"

"I don't know how. I'll hurt you if I try." He shook his head and smiled at her. "Are you going to help me or not? I'm so close now that I want to touch myself so I can get relief."

"Christ." He fucked her again and again, his cock not just filling her but becoming a part of her until she felt her pussy tighten again. She felt him lick her throat, and then he looked at her again. "Think of biting me. Christ, hurry. I'm going to come as soon as you sink your teeth into me."

She felt them then. Her mouth hurt for all of a second, then she felt the need to bite him. He told her to lick his throat until she could feel his pulse, then to bite.

"Bite me hard. And when you do, your mouth will fill and I want you to suck me down." He was pounding into her now, his cock touching her so deep she knew that tomorrow she'd be sore. When he licked her again she did the same to his throat and felt the pounding pulse. Sinking her fangs into him she felt him do the same. Clar came apart with a scream as soon as he drew at her throat.

Nothing could have ever prepared her for the way his blood felt going down the back of her throat. The taste alone was enough to take her over the edge, and when she drew at his throat, taking more of him into her, she came again, her body falling over the edge of a great cliff before she lifted up, only to fall again and again. When he threw back his head, tearing his mouth from her neck and her mouth from him, she dug her nails into his arms as another, more powerful climax gripped her. As she tumbled over into it, she screamed out his name even as he pulled her to him and bit her again. Clar felt the darkness reach up and jerk her into it. And she knew when she woke, if she did, nothing would ever be the same.

Chapter 9

"What do you think of this one?" Clar looked at the shirt and felt herself cringe from it. Gab laughed and hung it back on the rack. "I guess you're not into that much color. Me either if you want the truth."

Clar turned from the rack of shirts and decided that there was no one ready for that much color. She thought of the amount of pinks and yellows that had gone into the material and wondered if that was why it was so expensive. A single shirt should never cost eighty-five dollars.

"I don't know why we're doing this." Clar looked at Kennedy and Thor as they rummaged through the stacks of blue jeans and piled them onto the lady who was helping them. "I could have done well with going to some second-hand place and picking up a pair or two of pants and a few tee-shirts."

"You could have, I suppose, but what fun would that have been?" Gab handed her a navy blue blouse that looked like it was made of silk. She caught herself wondering if it would feel as good as Stephen's shirts had on her bare breasts, and glared when Gab laughed. "Yeah, been there a lot too."

"He makes me crazy." Gab nodded and put the blouse on the ever growing pile. "Have you ever known anyone who can say so much with just a single moan?"

"You have him moaning, do you? Well, that's always a good thing." Clar wanted to stomp her foot. "You should try having him howl. Jimmy can howl like nobody's business. Especially when he's in the moment."

Clar flushed again. These women had been talking like this since they'd picked her up this morning. Sex, sex, sex. She wondered if they thought of anything else. Clar had agreed to go out with Gab, but the rest had shown up when they'd gotten to the mall. It was an ambush, plain and simple.

"What do you think of your house?" Her house? Clar didn't have one and started to ask her what she meant when she continued. "I'd never been there before last week. I thought for some reason that it would be sort of smallish and all black and dark. Who knew he knew how to decorate?"

"*His* house is nice." Clar emphasized "his" because she didn't own a thing. The credit card he'd given her before she left had her name on it, which had surprised her, but she'd been rushed out the door before she could tell him no. And then there was the phone.

"You're ringing." She looked at Gab, who nodded to her waist. "I think either your ass is ringing or your cell phone is going off. Might want to answer it. Mates can be pissy if they can't reach out and touch you when they need to."

Pulling out the stupid thing, it took her another ring before she was able to answer it. She knew she was short to the caller, but was frustrated more than she could say. The person at the other end was quiet for so long she thought she'd hung up on them. Finally they hung up and she put the phone back.

You okay? She nearly cried out when Stephen spoke to her. He'd asked her last night not to block him anymore. She'd known she'd been doing it, but she'd been so sated when he'd woke her up by bringing her to another climax that she was sure he'd done it on purpose.

Someone is calling me and not talking. And did you know that there are three women with me and not just Gab? And also, they took me to a boutique, not to a used clothing place like I'd asked to be taken to. She blew her bangs out of her eyes and felt her frustration begin to build. *Why am I doing this?*

As much as I love having you naked all the time, where I can come up behind you and bend you over whatever is close, I think Kasen would be embarrassed. Clar felt her face heat up because Stephen had bent her over a chair and taken her that way when she'd gotten up to shower. Then he'd taken her in the shower while she'd been in there, as well as back to bed when they'd dried off. She was either going to be broken when he got tired of her or worn the hell out all the time.

You do know that I can hear your thoughts now, right? He laughed, and she did stomp her foot this time. *I'm not going to break you. I might wear you out, but that's fun too. And I'm not going to get tired of you. I know we have things to discuss, but we're together now. Forever.*

How long is forever to you? She wanted to take the words back as soon as she said them, but knew she couldn't. Clar wasn't used to this, people and him, especially him. She wanted things to slow down, take it easy.

You know how long forever is. She had expected him to be pissed, but he didn't sound like it. And that was another thing. He'd changed, and she wasn't sure what to make of it. *What do you mean, I'm different? Is it a good thing, you think?*

I don't know. You're...I know this sounds mean, but you're being nice to me. Why? You got what you wanted. I'm sleeping with you. What little sleep we get, that is.

You think that's all I want...of course you do. And why not? I've been a real bastard, but I promise you I'm going to change. Not because I want to fuck you, but because I want to make love to you. She told him she didn't love him. *And that's all right too. We'll just learn to like each other first. And if it happens, it happens. I would very much like to make it up to you, all the things I've done to hurt you. And I know that I have.*

I do like... She looked around the room and felt something. Looking at the other women, she knew that Thor felt it too because she came toward her with her hand on her gun. Even Gab had tensed up. *Someone is making us very nervous.*

Where are you? Are the other women with you? She told him they were rounding up the wagons now. *I'm sending Samuel and Jimmy. I can't come to you yet.*

Okay. She had no idea why, but she did feel better that someone was going to help out. There was something out there, and she had no idea what it was. *Send Vinnie too. I'm not sure why, but I think...Stephen? What does your vamp look like?*

Christ. Blonde with dark eyes. I don't remember what the actual color is, but dark. She's tall and wears heels that make her look taller. Small breasts that she for some reason displays when she's out. It wasn't her, which she should have known because it was light out. *I'm coming to you.*

Don't. If I need you to rescue us, then I need you to be healthy. Gab handed her a gun, and she put it in the back of her pants. *I'm armed now.*

She saw him before he saw her. Her stepfather was talking to a group of men as well as a female vamp, and pointing in different directions in the upscale mall. Clar wondered how the vamp could be out during the day when Stephen couldn't. Clar looked at Kennedy when she said it was wolf blood that was helping her. Clar told Stephen everything.

She's not a full blood. Probably changed by a made vampire too. That would be my guess as to why she can be out during the daylight. But she has to be in pain no matter what her breed is. The sun hurts all of us on some level. She told him thanks. *Look at your stepfather. Is he burning too?*

He was. His skin looked red and blistered. He kept wiping it with a handkerchief as well. And she realized he'd lost a great deal of weight. Moving into his mind, she found more information than she wanted, but decided to think about it later. Right now they had to get the hell out of there before someone got hurt.

I think he knows we're here. Not which shop, but that we're here. Stephen growled, and she laughed. *It's not like I can't take him, and with these other women here, I'm pretty sure we can take the wolves as well.*

I wish I could be there. She found she wanted him there too. *That's the nicest thing you've ever said to me, other than you liked sucking my dick. I enjoyed that as well. I'm getting hard just thinking about it.*

Are you trying to distract me? He laughed. *Stop it. I have to think. There has to be a way for us to get out of here without anyone getting hurt. I just have to think a minute.*

The woman who had been hovering around them since they'd walked in came up to her. Clar knew she was a cat but not what kind. She smiled at her and let enough of herself go that Clar knew she was a panther. She led them to the back room.

"I'll hold your things and have them sent to the house for you. Samuel called and told me to see if I could get you out of here, or at least somewhere safe until he arrived."

Clar moved to the door with the other three and to the service door. "An alarm will sound, but by the time security gets here, you'll be long gone."

"Thank you." Kennedy hugged the younger woman and spoke to her for just a minute longer. When she was finished, they pushed open the heavy door and were in the lot just as a large SUV came to a screeching halt in front of them. The man was out and had her before she could think to fight him. When he squeezed her tight and said her name, she stilled.

"My name is Hawk, and I'm going to let you go now. Will you try not to hurt me?" His laughter bubbled out as he continued. "Vinnie said you were a hellion. Come on and get in. I've orders to take you to one of the offices downtown."

The ride was made a little more bearable because Kennedy had them all laughing. She wasn't sure why they thought some of the things she was saying was funny, but then Clar didn't have a lot of interaction with other women. And that saddened her for some reason. Clar didn't join in too much because all she could think about was she could have gotten any or all of them hurt. And the fact that Edward was going to use her as bait. Just as they stopped, Kennedy hit her in the head with the palm of her hand.

"You think you're the only one with these super powers?" She started to tell her she didn't have any when she hit her again. "You healed my mother-in-law. If that doesn't qualify for super power, then I don't know what does."

"He wants to turn me over to the vamp that wants to kill Stephen." Kennedy nodded and pulled her to her for a hug. For the first time in a very long time, Clar welcomed the touch. But she did pull away first. "I don't want to get anyone hurt."

"Then see that you don't. Come on in. They've rounded up the troops, and there is even some food if I don't miss my bet." Kennedy laughed as she got out of the big car. "I'm always hungry, it seems. Must be all the sex."

Rolling her eyes, Clar got out. She'd either have to think of things to say that wouldn't embarrass her, or simply figure out a way to blush less. She doubted anything would help that.

~~~

Stephen wanted to take her into his arms and tell her that things would be all right. But they wouldn't, not until this was settled. He was ready to get up and tell the family he and Clarice were going back to the house when Summer came to stand in front of him. He asked her if she wanted his seat.

"Oh heavens no. I don't think I've sat for more than ten minutes since she touched me. You've no idea what a pleasure I find in having my legs tired and my feet achy from walking too much." He stood up anyway. "I'd very much like to take a walk. Would you accompany me?"

He looked at Clar, who had been sitting in the same chair since he'd gotten there an hour after they had. She'd spoke to him, but he could tell she was distracted. And no matter how hard he tried, she'd blocked him out again. Kennedy had asked him to let her work it out. She was scared shitless, and she needed time. Moving to her, he touched her cheek and she looked at him with a glassy look.

"I'm going to take a walk." She nodded and smiled at him, but made no effort to stand. He'd hoped she'd ask to go with him, but she only looked away again and seemed to zone out. Stephen went with Summer to the yard just behind the offices they were in.

"Have you told her yet?" Stephen looked at Summer, wondering if he'd missed something in her conversation. "Clar, have you told her that you love her yet?"

"I don't love her." He'd answered too quickly and they both knew it. "I don't. We're just working out being together without wanting to kill each other. Neither of us is in love."

"If you say so." Stephen nodded at her, but he didn't think she believed him. "Did she tell you that this Edward person wants to use her as bait to get you? He plans to turn you over to Velvet."

She'd not told him, but he'd figured it out. Why else would he take a bunch of wolves to a mall in the daylight but to get her? What he was trying to figure out was how he'd known she was going to be there. His mind drifted to Summer's original question.

"I don't love her. Why did you ask me that?" She looked at him and shook her head. "Is it only hopeful thinking? Did she ask you to see if I loved her? No, that wouldn't be like her, she'd ask me herself."

"She would. Then give you a good kick in the butt if it wasn't the answer she thought it should be." Stephen smiled, knowing she was correct. "You don't love her, so what does it matter why I thought so?"

"I don't." He felt stupid when he said it that way. His tone had been sharp and he'd not meant it to be. "She doesn't much care for me either. The only reason we're together is because...well, we sort of have a mutual interest right now."

"You mean sex." Stephen flushed, and he felt like he was ten again. "It's all right, Stephen, I know a little about sex and mates. But sex isn't everything."

"It's not, but it's all we have." He felt his heart take a funny twist, and he rubbed it before continuing. "Does she think that I'll turn her over to Barron? She doesn't, does she?"

"Not that I'm aware of. She talked a little with Kennedy on the way here, but then she sort of shut down. I think she's a very deep thinker." Summer walked to the edge of the lot, then turned back to him. "Did you know that she healed me with just a touch of her finger? Ran it up and down my arm of all places and told me to get out of my chair. I thought Kennedy was going to kick her ass. You've no idea after all this time what it was like to wiggle my toes."

He did know what it was like to be free. And he was sure that was what Summer had meant. "Why do you think I love her?"

Stephen had no idea why that bothered him so much, but it did. He didn't love her, damn it. And she didn't love him. Summer gave him that smile that said "you're just a big dumb animal, aren't you?"

"Why do you not love her?" He was startled by the reverse question and shook his head. Why indeed?

"We were thrown together because of some chemical need for each other and nothing more. Why more people don't just...why do we even have this gene in us, anyway? What if I was perfectly happy with being alone and single? Maybe I liked my solitary life."

"Did you?" Summer didn't wait for him to answer, but started back to the house. "I'm going in. I think they're going to start moving everyone to the house soon, and I want to be there to see that dinner is big enough."

"They're coming to my house." He flushed when she looked at him. "Our house. They're coming to our house, and Kasen has brought in some extra help so that there will be plenty for everyone to eat. I think he's rather enjoying himself."

"So he would." She moved into the house and he stood there. It was still light enough that he could feel the waning sun on his face, but not enough to burn him. Stephen let the sounds around him lull him into a trance, and he tried to find Velvet. He was sure she had made it so that her home was warded against any kind of magic he could use to find her, but he tried anyway. He opened his eyes when someone touched him.

"I can help you." He nodded at Clarice and her fingers moved up his neck and to his head. The connection was profound and strong. He reached out again and found her.

"She's at rest. And Ted, her day walker, is beside her." He reached into Velvet's mind and found it to be blank. So she did it the old fashioned way and shut down completely. Stephen only rested, his mind alert to his surroundings. It was dangerous the way she was doing it, but extremely helpful to him. Her way made her easy prey to anyone looking for her.

"The man is dead." Stephen moved to Ted and found that Clarice was right; he was indeed dead and not just resting. Someone had torn out his throat.

"She did it at her rest. If a vampire goes to rest without feeding or feeding well, they can wake hungry. It's not uncommon in vampires like her." Clar asked him what made her different from him. "She's an animal."

He couldn't find an address, but he'd found enough clues to figure out where they were. Before he could pull away from Clarice to break the connection, she moved them through the house and into another mind. It was Edward.

It took him a few minutes to sort out his memories. They were disjointed and full of fear. Twice he'd had to have Clarice slow down as she was moving through them much faster than he'd been able to. She'd had a great deal more practice, he knew, but she was helping him, and that mattered a great deal. And when they paused on a dark night, neither of them moved.

He was seeing it as Edward was seeing it, he realized. Edward was nervous, and he kept looking around as if whatever was going on or about to happen was going to be bad. It made Stephen sort of nauseous, but he felt Clarice tighten her grip on his mind, and he settled down. When a car stopped not five feet from him, Edward moved toward it but stayed in the shadows.

It was quick. The ball bat that another man held was smashed into the driver's window as soon as he came to the car. The driver was disabled immediately, but it was the passenger that had his full attention. It was a younger Clarice. She was screaming at her mother to drive, but it was too late. Edward moved closer to the car, looking up and down the street twice more before he looked down at the older woman. Her head had been beaten in, and brains and blood stained the road. When Edward walked around to the other side of the car, he saw something and was frightened by it. Stephen knew what it had been; it was the faeries that had been with them that night. As he walked around the car, Clarice had been dragged out of it at some point and was trying to crawl away. Her arm and legs had been beaten, and her face was covered in blood. Edward was handed the bat, and he swung it upward. Before it came down, the memory stopped, and Stephen opened his eyes.

"He did it." She nodded. "How long have you known? And what have you told the police?"

"I didn't know...I knew, I think, that he'd been a part of my mother's death, but not that he'd actually been there. I had no idea that he'd...he tried to kill me." He pulled her into his arms and held her as she sobbed. "He hit me with the bat and...and he killed me."

"The faeries saved you that night. I could see them working on you when I touched the scar. It's why you can read minds so well. All of our minds." She nodded, and he tightened his hold on her when she started to pull away. "Just give me a little more time. I need this even if you don't."

He held her for as long as he could, but they were outside without much in the way of protection and needed to get moving. He took her hand and looked into her eyes. Nothing in the world could have prepared him for what he felt. He wasn't just in love with her, but he needed her as well.

"Can you show me how to do that moving thing?" He frowned, not really understanding. "You know, how you take us somewhere without really moving?"

"We move, but very fast." He didn't know if she could do it or not, because he'd never converted her, but he thought if she wanted to try, he'd do anything for her. "Close your eyes and think of where you want to be. You have to think of the room too, not just the place. It won't do us any good if we end up in a piece of furniture or something like a door."

"That's why when I move the table in the living room, Kasen puts it back." She laughed. "And the chairs in the kitchen are always around the table and not pulled out. I understand now."

Stephen was impressed that she'd even noticed. He knew that she was very neat and tidy about her things, but he'd not realized how observant she was. When she told him she had it, he felt the air around them tighten. In the next breath they were both standing in the kitchen of their home. Kasen turned to look at them.

"There are six wolves in the dining room, sire, as well as three more in the pantry. I have taken the liberty of having a large grill brought in to replace the one that came with the household. I do believe it was rusted beyond use anyway." He looked at Clarice and smiled. "You did well, my lady. It will be nothing for you to pop to the store and back for me should you require something for lunch I do not have."

"You knew it was me?" He smiled. "How? I mean, I thought I did really well, but if I missed something, it would be good to know."

"The master does not come to the kitchen unless he knows where I am. I might have been in your way." She nodded, and Kasen looked at him again. "We have a visitor on the grounds, sire, and he is most not welcome."

"Who?" Kasen looked out the window over the sink then at him again. Whoever it was, Kasen was not happy about it.

"The police, sire. They arrived about an hour ago. I have kept them from the household grounds, but they have made their way into the woods. I was afraid to have the wolves go out and scare them off. I feared they'd shoot them."

"Let them hang out. In a little while, we'll have Vinnie go out and shift. If that doesn't run them off, nothing will." Kasen smiled. "We might have Samuel and Kennedy go out too. They were just saying they needed a good run."

"Very good, sire. My lady, packages have arrived for you. I have put them on the bed for you to sort through. It looks as if you had a very productive day." She looked at him, then at Kasen.

"I didn't buy anything." She moved out of the kitchen, and he followed. He wondered what the hell was going on. As soon as he entered their bedroom, he stopped. She had had a productive day. There must have been two hundred bags in the room.

"Are we broke?" He was kidding her, but she looked so stricken that he went to her. "I'm kidding, love, honestly. If you bought the mall, we'd have more than enough money to live on for the rest of our days. What on earth did you do, speed shop?"

He picked up the first bag he reached and looked inside. Whatever it was looked like silk and lace. Pulling it out, he nearly swallowed his tongue before she jerked it from him.

"I most certainly did not purchase this." He reached for another bag and held it over her head so he could pull whatever was in it out. This one was green, dark, and luscious.

"Please tell me you plan to model this for me." She glared at him, but he could see the lust starting to take over her anger. "Why don't you go and put it on now? I'll wait."

"It's a bra." Stephen nodded. "What on earth could be so sexy about a bra? I suppose you want me to put the matching panties on as well?"

He nodded again and felt the overwhelming desire to wipe his chin. He was hungry for her, and she was finally getting it. Taking the bag from him, she moved to the bathroom, but stopped before she entered.

"Here's what's going to happen. I'm going to put this on and you're going to go downstairs to entertain the guests you invited here." He shook his head. "Yes you are, and if you're really good, I'll try on the things I found in the other bag. I do believe it's sheer. And black too."

"You're going to pay for this." She nodded and smiled. "Christ, I'm not going to be able to concentrate on anything wondering what the fuck you're wearing…or not wearing."

"You might want to wear a longer shirt too. Your cock is showing." He rubbed his hand over his painful erection, and she smiled at him. "I'm very wet."

"Fuck them." Stephen moved to her, and she squealed. The door slammed in his face and he nearly broke it down. But what he heard on the other side made his heart pound. She was laughing. Stephen was sure if there was a more beautiful musical sound, he'd never heard it. He told her he'd be downstairs and moved out of the room before he did something he wanted to do when they were alone, like tell her that he was in love with her.

Chapter 10

He's dead, he's dead, he's dead kept rolling though his mind over and over as Edward swept up the ash. He'd been told to come down here to clean up the mess just after he'd gotten home. He'd no idea it was going to be a body. Then…then it was ash.

"I told you it'd be easy to do. You should have brought down that sweeper thing. It's handheld, and it does a good job of cleaning up the mess." Edward looked at Velvet, stunned at her attitude. "What? It's not like he was my mate or anything. We just enjoyed each other's bodies for a time. Now you'll have me all to yourself."

Not a thought that made him feel good. Edward had been trying for days to figure out how to get out of this mess he was in, and now that Ted was dead, she'd been talking more about converting him too. He didn't want to be a fucking vampire.

"You will need to feed me soon." He felt his body get clammy. That meant sex too. And as much as he enjoyed it while it was happening, he didn't want to have sex with her any more. Ever again. "I'm willing to wait until you've had a chance to shower. I can't stand the smell of dead vamp, and you positivity reek of it."

KATHI S. BARTON

"You killed him." She smiled and nodded. "Didn't you love him at all? I mean, weren't you guys together for a while?"

"Yeah, so? Like I said, he wasn't my mate, so it matters little. He knew the risks when he slept with me. When I get hungry, I just leap for the throat." He felt his balls and cock seem to crawl up into his body when she licked her lips and stared at his cock. "You will need to eat more. I tend to get very hungry when I'm hunting. It's why I always have two in my bed when I fuck someone."

Two. Two more bodies he'd have to clean up after if…he looked at the door longingly when she got up to leave the room. He wanted out. And right now, dead was preferable over living like this. But he was a coward. He knew that as well as Velvet probably did. He put the dust pan on the trash can and made his way to the kitchen.

They were all gone. As of the day before, when he'd returned from the mall, the household staff had disappeared. When he'd asked Velvet about them, she'd only shrugged. He had a feeling that they were much like the man in the basement, dead. But he'd found a note in the kitchen early this morning and he felt slightly relieved.

"There are all manner of meats in the freezer. I would suggest you begin eating red meat, rare at every meal, including breakfast." Edward had sat down to finish reading when he realized why the butler was telling him this. "We have moved to another estate to prepare it for her arrival. She believes when she finishes here, she will need to lay low for a while. I do hope you get what you deserve."

Edward was pretty sure he was, too.

The mall had been a bust. His information had been correct, of course, but Kelley had left before he could find her. The wolves he'd had looking for her to come there had called him the moment she'd gotten out of the large stretch limo with the other women. It had only been on his list of places to look for just over an hour.

Edward had thought of the way she'd looked, his stepdaughter, in the picture he'd seen of her. He'd spoken to Hump twice more since that day, and both times the man had told him that if he didn't get some money soon, then Edward was getting no more information. And he assured Edward that what he had was vital to what he wanted. Edward was pretty sure he was going to tell him something he already knew, but the man might have something. He'd made an appointment to talk to him again today while Velvet was awake. She said she'd get what he wanted.

Edward looked around the kitchen and the mess. He'd never had to cook for himself before, and his first attempt at making himself a steak had ended badly. He glanced at the burn marks up the wall and the countertop that had suffered as well, and wondered if Velvet would even notice. As far as he could tell, she'd never been in this room, at least not since he'd known her. But he'd eaten it all the same, terrified of being drained by her when she woke.

He looked at his reflection in the window over the door. He looked…he didn't look thin, but looked like a man who had been very ill for a very long time. And he'd weighed himself yesterday morning and nearly cried. Before Velvet he'd weighed two hundred and ten pounds. Not really fat, but he'd been overweight for his six foot two frame. Now he weighed one twenty-five. Only half his former weight. He looked gaunt, his eyes were sunk back in his head, and his hair was falling out. Then there were the open wounds.

When she'd gone down on him after she'd gotten up, Ted had remarked on the ones on his back as well. Edward had been itchy but didn't know there were wounds. Velvet said there were two on his dick and that she'd done it. He had looked after they'd all had sex and sure enough, she'd bitten him. And when he'd looked at his back, those too looked like bite marks. Ted had found him looking at them.

"She's marking you. For that matter, so am I. I kind of like the way it looks on you." He asked him why. "So nobody will want you. But I'd ask her to lay off if I were you. If you don't let her convert you soon, she's going to do it anyway. Those bites are deep, and if they become too infected, as in you're dying from them, she can convert you without your permission or let you die."

She was killing him so she could do what she'd been telling him she was going to do for days now. According to the butler, she needed his permission to change him. Or if not that, then he'd have to be dying. Right now it was a toss-up if he was going to make it until he could get out before she did what she wanted.

"You should know that I'm going to bring in another partner. I can't have you getting it in your head that you're the only one for me." Velvet shoved him back on the chair and sat on his lap. He'd not even heard her come in the room. "It's time to feed me."

The bite to his throat had him screaming. Edward tried to pull her off him, but she wrapped her arms around his head and held him to her mouth. He could feel the life draining out of him and thought he'd welcome it. Darkness took him away smiling.

When he woke, it was dark in the room. He'd never been one to be afraid of the darkness, but the cold seeping into his body was more than he could stand. Moving slightly, he realized where he was and who was beside him, and her body was as cold as death. And he knew that's just what she was. Death. Then he thought of where he was. Christ, she'd taken him to her lair.

"I will rest easily tonight, but in the future it will be your job to protect me." Edward didn't say anything because he wasn't sure he could open his mouth without screaming. "From now on, until I turn you, you'll sleep with me. Then when the time is right I'll make you like me."

"I don't—" She cut him off with a low growl and he swallowed twice before continuing. "I will protect you. You won't...you won't kill me, will you? If you wake in the night, you won't kill me, right?"

She yawned and sank her teeth into his shoulder, and Edward felt his cock harden. The fucking monster didn't know when enough was enough. When she reached down to fondle him, Edward knew that as soon as he could get to the kitchen, he was cutting his throat. No amount of money in the world was worth what he was going through right now. When he came, she rolled on top of him and a light flared behind her body, silhouetting her for him. He couldn't see her face well, but enough to know that her fangs were long and sharp right now. They got longer the angrier and the hungrier she got.

"You do anything stupid and I will be very pissed at you. I've enough of your blood right now that if you were to try and cut your throat to spite me, I'd feel it and save you by turning you anyway. You understand what I'm telling you?" He nodded. "Good boy. Now, stick that cock in me and let me ride you until I come. I'm very horny right now."

His cock was so painfully hard that he wasn't surprised when he came three times before she fell atop him. Rolling her to his side, he lay there for a long time thinking about what the fuck had happened to him. He had no one to blame but himself. Her, too, of course, but there was little to nothing he could do about that now. He was as good as dead or a fucking vampire. He didn't let himself think of killing himself, but did plan to confront Silva. As soon as the man killed him, the better Edward would feel about the world in general. The sun was nearly set when he finally closed his eyes. Today he'd figure out how to get out of this shit.

~~~

Clar moved down the stairs the next morning a little slower than she thought she would. He'd been an animal last night, and she decided that she'd never hold him off again. Well, maybe she would, but not for long. He'd torn her clothes from her in the front hall before the last car was out of the driveway.

"Mine," he'd told her when she tried to get away from him, but he held her. "I'm going to take you here, and if you make a sound, Kasen will watch his master fucking his mate."

"Please, let's go up to the bedroom." He growled as he pulled her shirt off her. The bra and panty set made her feel sexy, and the way he looked at her then, she thought maybe she might buy the store out. He'd looked…hungry.

"No." Her pants had come off next. He tossed them away from her as he stood in front of her, staring. Clar had felt her pussy soaking the panties and tried to squeeze her legs together to stop it. "Let me see. Open your legs and let me see just how wet I've made you."

Trembling, she did as he said. He didn't move closer to her, but she could feel him touching her as if he were. She moaned when she felt his fingers slide over her belly, and knew that he was doing this to her with his mind. When she reached between her legs to touch herself, her arms were suddenly above her head.

"I told you, this is mine." His two steps toward her made her wetter. By the time he was an inch from her, she was panting. Her body wasn't on fire for him, but a living, breathing flame. His shirt had disappeared, and she licked her lips. The need to taste him was making her want to beg.

"Don't make a sound." She nodded, not sure that was going to be possible when he dropped in front of her. He touched her thighs with the lightest of touches, and she danced on her feet, trying to get some relief. "You can come, but you'll be quiet about it. If you call down the staff, I'll be most displeased with you."

"Make me come." He pulled her panties down to her thighs and kissed the area just above her pussy. "Stephen, please don't tease me. You have been doing this all night."

He had too. Every time he had come near her he'd touch her in some way, brush against her breast, and cup her ass. It wasn't long after they had dinner started that he started sending her images of them together. Of her riding him again, his cock in her mouth while she sucked him. She heard herself screaming at the top of her lungs when she'd come, her begging him to fuck her. By the time their company had started making noises about leaving, she was ready to beg them to leave, wanting to help them to their cars.

His tongue played with her clit. She bit her lips to try to keep from screaming, but when he suckled her into his mouth, she couldn't help it. A cry of pleasure spilled out before she could stop it. He lifted his head and looked up at her.

"Come." She came apart, her body let go without him even touching her this time. Before she was finished, another one grabbed her hard and she screamed again. This time she was in their room and he had her on the bed. Her arms and legs were tied to the bed.

"I'm going to play with you." And he had. To the point where she wasn't just begging him to give her what she needed, but promising him whatever he'd wanted. "Anything?"

"Yes. Please, anything. Just let me come. Please, I'm begging you." He lifted her up and rolled her over his legs, the ties at her limbs suddenly gone. She thought for sure he'd been going to take her from behind, but he slapped her ass hard enough that she came up off his lap in seconds. "What the hell was that for?"

"Come here, Clarice, and let me have my fun. If you do, I'll give you so much pleasure you'll faint with it." He lay back on the bed and his clothes were suddenly gone. He wrapped his hand around his cock and began stroking himself. "Would you like to ride me again?"

"Yes." Her mouth watered for the chance to take him into her mouth and she moved forward.

"Not yet. What I want from you is to cause you just a little pain. Not much, but just a little."

"Why?" He continued to play with his cock, and she watched as a stream of his cum slipped from the opening to his balls. "Let me suck on you now and I'll let you spank me."

"Will you let me change you? Not tonight, but soon? I want to be able to give you what I am. I want to be able to not worry that I should be safe with you." She'd looked at him then. "I hold back because even though we've come so close to you being like me, you are still human."

"You want me to be a vampire?" He nodded. "I won't know how to...I don't think I could feed from anyone but you."

"And you shan't. You're mine. And as my mated vampire, I will be the only one you feed from and I from you. Forever. If you touch another man, for any reason, I will kill him. I am a very jealous man. There may be times when you will have to feed from someone else, but you'll need to be marked again by me, and I will try to restrain my natural need to kill. I'll take you hard and bite you so that his scent, his taste will be gone." She stood there and waited, knowing there was more. "There is. You will be hurt for me to do this. Mortally wounded so that my blood will change you. It's the way all vampires do it, but because I'm a pureblood, you'll be as strong as me and have the benefits that I have."

"Such as?" She wasn't sure she wanted to be a vampire, but she was willing to listen. When he sat up, she came to him when he told her to. After she was on the bed, her knees planted firmly beneath her, she moaned when he came up behind her.

"You'll be able to take me like this." His cock filled her. She cried out with his girth; it was so much thicker than she remembered. "I'm inside of you as my beast. Do you feel him?" She did too. It was more than his cock, but his body felt colder, his skin tighter.

Looking at his hands as he held himself over her, she could see his nails. They were long and thick, claws almost. Clarice wondered aloud if he'd positioned her this way so she couldn't see his face.

"I have. You're afraid enough." He moved in and out of her, and soon she was backing into his thrusts. "You're going to make me come if you keep that up, and I want to make this last. I've never taken a woman this way before. When I bite you, it will be painful, I'm afraid. But if you'd prefer that I not, say so."

"Please." She'd barely gotten the word out when he pulled from her body and rolled her to her back. Clar could see him now, and she knew what the real meaning of vampire meant. He was right in front of her.

"I won't harm you." She nodded, and he slid between her thighs with his body. The different angle gave her a little discomfort but not much. When he was settled over her body, she looked into his bloodied eyes. "You're beautiful."

"Bite me. Please, I want to come around you." His head lowered slowly, she was sure to give her time to change her mind. She'd seen his fangs; they were long and sharp, sharper than she'd ever seen them. When he licked her throat, his tongue felt rough and hot. As soon as his teeth dug into her, she came, screaming out his name even as he pounded her hard enough to hurt.

He came moments later. His hot cum seemed to not just fill her, but to cover her as well. Holding him to her body, she came twice more before he lifted his head and stared down at her. Tilting her neck again, she waited for him to finish her.

"You're sure?" She nodded. And when he tore at her throat, she knew a moment of panic, then nothing. Clar knew that for the first time in her life she was safe in another person's care.

"My lady." Clar looked at Kasen and wondered if he'd been talking to her for long. She'd been so lost in what had happened last night she'd completely zoned out. "Would you care to try something to eat?"

"You know." He nodded and moved ahead of her. Clar followed because she was hungry, and curious to know how he'd figured it out when she wasn't even sure it had worked. "I think I can eat. The thought of something meaty comes to mind. No veggies."

He moved around the kitchen while she tried her best to figure out how to word it. He sat a plate of steak and ham and bacon in front of her and she looked at him. He sat down, something she'd never seen him do since she'd been staying there.

"You're curious, I can see." She nodded as she picked up a slice of bacon and ate it. "You smell different. And there is an air about you that says that you are no longer human. I think it suits you very well."

"Then why am I eating this and wondering if you have any more?" He smiled and stood up, putting more sliced ham in the skillet. She heard it sizzle and crack and wondered if he could hurry the process up. "Kasen, I'm like really hungry."

"Come here." Stephen was sudden standing between her and Kasen, and she went to him. As soon as he touched her, she took his throat. The feeling of his blood going down the back of her throat had her moaning. He simply held her to him until she lifted her head. She felt not quite full, but not nearly as hungry as she'd been before.

"Better?"

"Yes. I was…you thought I was going to bite him, didn't you?" He nodded. "I wouldn't have. I was going to ask him if that was normal to be this starved, but you showed up. Would he have known what to do?"

"He would have called for me. But I felt your hunger first." She sat down, suddenly dizzy. "Your body is adjusting. You'll be fine in a couple of days. In the meantime you'll have to drink more than you did before, and not leave the house unless I'm with you. I don't want you to hurt anyone. Not that I think you will, but there will be times when you need more than you can eat."

"Will I? Hurt someone, I mean." He shrugged and picked up a slice of bacon and handed it to her. She noticed that the skillet was off the burner and that Kasen was gone. "I scared him, didn't I?"

"I don't think so. He left while you were busy." She flushed. She'd wanted more than his blood. She'd wanted him and she was pretty sure he knew it. But she wanted answers first.

"Kasen said he could smell I was no longer human. Will all humans be able to smell that? And will I have to carry around blood so I won't eat everyone I see?" He laughed, and she wanted to smack him. But Kasen came back in the room then and started cooking. "I'm sorry, Kasen. I would never have hurt you."

"Not to worry, my lady. You are newly turned and you will have some things to work out. Had I known that you'd not fed before coming down, I would have called his lordship to you." He put another plate of food in front of her. "I do believe I will have to order a deep freezer as well as hire a few more staff members to run the house, my lady. You will need someone to care for you as well as the house. You will be very busy I believe."

"Busy?" Kasen looked at Stephen, who was looking like he'd been told he was getting no dessert. "What is he talking about, and how pissed am I going to be with you?"

"Very, I'm thinking. And I should have mentioned this last night but you...distracted me." He kissed her nose after pulling her to his lap. "I'm the master in this area, and as of the morning you killed Jared, I am the highest *acting* member of the Vampire Council. Which means you are as well. We have over five hundred subjects."

She looked at him to see if he was kidding and could see that he wasn't. "What the hell am I supposed to do with five hundred subjects? Whatever that means. And I didn't distract you as much as you did me, vamp boy."

He swatted her ass when she stood up, and she moved away from him when she threw her water in his face. His laughter made her want to tease him more, make him smile at her as he was doing right now.

All movement came to a halt when someone knocked on the back door. Clar felt something in her rise up, and she heated with anger when she saw who was there. Snatching the door open and nearly off the hinges, she glared at Edward.

"What the fuck are you doing here? I should kill you right now." He dropped to his knees, and she looked at Stephen.

"Please do it. Make it quick before she finds me." He looked behind him as if someone might pop out at any minute. "Invite me in."

She looked at Stephen, then back at Edward. There was no fucking way she was letting this fucking bastard into her life, much less this house. But before she could tell him no or something a good deal harsher, he laughed.

"Fortunately for me, they don't need an invitation." The door snapped from her fingers as wolves, at least a dozen of them, forced their way in. She fell back as the first one hit her. Pain radiated from her head, but she sat up. Before she could move to defend herself, she felt something hit her…netting. Stephen cried out as he, too, was covered. Then a pain in her head took her breath away, and everything went black.

Chapter 11

Velvet looked at her prize. She had to refrain from dancing around him every time she looked at Stephen. The man was finally where she wanted him to be...tied to the chair and at her mercy. Well, she'd already decided that she'd show him none. Why should she when he'd never shown her the least amount when she'd needed it? But the girl...she wished now that she'd not promised Eddie he could have her.

It was his mate. Who would have thought that he'd find one after all this time, and her a vampire too? She hadn't been one when she'd lived with Eddie, but now she was pretty powerful. Velvet wondered how long she'd been changed and had to fight the urge to go into the other cell and tear her head off her shoulders. But if she was honest with herself, she was curious as to what Eddie would do with her.

He'd been jabbering for two days about getting her. Eddie had this plan, but it was stupid and she'd told him so several times. Then he'd come up with the idea of him going to the house and being invited in. After that, Velvet could find them by zeroing in on him. She didn't tell him she'd known where Stephen was for a few days now, because to do so would have meant admitting she was afraid to go to the house. It was being watched.

Velvet knew that Stephen was a powerful vampire and that he'd been a master of his own domain since he'd taken it from another vampire who had...well, she'd been sloppy and been caught fucking up. Velvet knew the other woman, had even come to admire her in some ways, but Valda had been too greedy and had tried to get things to run her way too soon. And then Stephen had also been in the way. When someone moved behind her, she turned.

"She's awake." Velvet nodded at Eddie and waited for him to continue. "She won't fucking speak to me. No matter what I do to her either."

"You've hit her?" He nodded, then shook his head. "You're starting to piss me off, you know. Not a good thing when I hold all the keys to your release."

That got his attention. "You said you'd release me if I got you Stephen. I held up my end of the bargain. You can't pull out now."

She was across the room before he could blink. If he had thought about it, he might have remembered he could move fast too, but she had him around the throat and a foot off the floor before he did anything. She let her beast go and stared at him.

"You'll do well to remember who is master here. I will say how long you'll stay and if you get to leave me. For now...for now you serve a purpose. When that purpose is served, I will release you from it." Eddie nodded, but she could see that his beast had risen too. She wanted to be impressed, but she was more pissed than anything. With a hard slam against the wall, she dropped him. "Now go to your little girl and either do what you want or give her to me. I'm sure I can find a usefulness about her that you'd never dream of."

Eddie left without a word. Velvet was having a hard time keeping him around in general lately. He was...bored, she supposed. The constant whining about his state of affairs or the lack of them, the way nothing was going as he wanted, and his absolute terror of becoming a vampire. Velvet had changed him just so he could see it wasn't all that bad. But that hadn't gone well either. Now he had something else to add to his list of woes. She shook her head and looked at her own pain in the ass and saw that he was awake and staring at her.

"You are mine now." He didn't move or even acknowledge her having him with any sound. "You think to pull the same shit on me as your darling mate is? Well, I got news for you. When I'm finished with you, you're going to be very sorry you let them bury me alive."

"You will pay for this." She felt her skin crawl at the calmness of the threat. He'd always had that way about him. He could deliver a threat or a promise in a way that had a person wanting to take it back the moment it was said. "And if you harm my mate, there will never be anywhere that I don't find you and tear your throat out."

"Big words for a man tied down with silver chains. How do you propose to do anything in the state you're in? Or do you expect some of the other animals you hang around with to come and save you?" She laughed at him, and she smiled at the way it echoed around the cavernous room. "They have no idea where you are and won't find you until it's too late. I plan to do to you what you had them do to me."

"Bury me in a silver casket." She nodded, though he didn't ask her a question. "Go ahead."

"You're over your fear of the dark now?" Velvet knew it was a lie the moment he nodded. "Bullshit. You're still a big fucking baby about it and we both know it. Your dear brother fucked you up, and I'm going to capitalize on that."

"You'll still pay. I will get out, and when I do, you're going to wish to Christ I'd kill you outright rather than what I want to do." Image after image of him tearing her to pieces flashed through her mind, her arms and legs being torn from her body while she still lived. In another set of images, he had her tied to a tree and the animals of the night tore at her flesh, wolves feasting on her bones while she screamed at them to stop. When she was being staked in the sun, her skin blistering up and festering, she could feel it…the heat of the sun, the tearing of her skin as it filled with blisters and they popped. Finally she moved to him and slapped him. His head jerked back. He turned and looked at her, and she saw death. And she knew it was her that was going to die.

"You think you're so superior, don't you?" He nodded at her, and she felt the urge to slap him again. When he lifted his chin for her, daring her to do as she wanted, Velvet walked to the door to leave. "I'm going to put you in my casket and bury you where no one will find you. And in a thousand years, I'll dig you up and stake you in the heart."

She started out the door, and he said her name softly. Velvet didn't want to turn; she didn't want to know what he was going to say, but she did and tried her best to avoid looking him in the eye. But she did and it was as if he'd captured her.

"You'd better hope it's a thousand years and that you're dead when they find me." She moved out of the room and stood in the hall with her back to the wall. She could hear his laughter as she tried to calm herself. He scared her more in this moment than when she'd been chained up and thrown into that hole. Shivering, she went to the other room to see how Eddie was faring.

He had more than just hit her. Eddie had beaten her so badly it was hard to tell what she might look like. Her hair was matted in blood, and her shirt front was saturated with it. She looked at Eddie, who was sitting in the corner staring at the girl. He was covered in blood, and his mouth was stained as well.

"You bit her?" He nodded and then dropped his head. Eddie needed to be watched since she'd changed him the day before yesterday. "Did you do it right?"

"Why does it matter? She's going to fucking die anyway." That was true, but he didn't get to play as long. "I'm going to bed. You can have her if I can't get her to talk when we get up."

She was going to take her anyway she decided, just looking at the way she sat there staring at them both as if she was so much better than them. Velvet went to the girl after Eddie left them and lifted her chin up to look. The wound at her throat was sealed, and her face was already healing.

"You think you're going to live through this?" The girl jerked from her grasp and smiled. It was so much like Stephen's had been that Velvet took a step back, which pissed her off more, and Velvet slapped her as well. "You're fucking going to die at the next rising. But before you do, I'm going to let Stephen fuck me while you watch. Won't you just love that, seeing your mate fucking a real woman?"

She said something, and Velvet leaned closer to hear her. "I said, when a real woman gets here, you let me know. I might pay to see that."

Velvet lost her temper. It was always on the verge lately anyway, but her rage didn't just spill out, but consumed her.

But when she reached for the girl, something happened. A barrier kept her from touching her, and no matter how hard she tried, she could not breach it.

"Who the hell is doing that?" Velvet looked around the room, even going as far as throwing the little bit of furniture toward the girl only to have it bounce back at her. "What the fuck is that?"

Nothing. There was not a sound from the girl, but she did smile. Velvet felt her fear again as it raced over her, and before she did something really stupid, like let her go, she left the room, slamming the door closed behind her. These two were going to die, and the sooner the better. Calling to her newest day walker, who, as far as she knew, hadn't told her his name, Velvet had the casket brought to the room where Stephen was.

"Put him in it, but don't unchain him. If you do, I will kill you and every single person that has the misfortune of being in your bloodline." He told her he would be careful. "I don't care if you're careful, you moron. I just don't want him free. Not ever."

Velvet went to their room and saw that Eddie had taken up most of the bed. Again. She was finished with him as well. He'd served her well, she supposed, and now...well, now she was done with his ass too. Going to the bedside table, she pulled out her dagger. Lifting it above her head, she came down with it in an arch and felt it as it broke bones to enter his heart.

Eddie opened his eyes as his life blood poured from him. Velvet watched as he stared at her, her body responding to his death as if he were fucking her hard. When he cried out, she did as well. A climax gripped her as hard as he had only hours before when he'd taken her in the ass.

Velvet held on to the bedpost while her body jerked and trembled with it. She felt euphoric, sated, and suddenly much energized by it. Moving his body off the bed and onto the floor, she lay on the saturated mattress and let the feeling of rest settle over her. Never had she had such a satisfying release as this.

"Maybe I need to kill someone nightly so that I can rest in peace." Laughing at her own double meaning, she closed her eyes and let her body go. She knew that when she rose again, she'd have the girl all to herself, and Stephen would be deep within the earth.

~~~

Clar felt his fear. She didn't understand it because her own was making her body quake with it. When she was able to calm her own pounding heart, she reached for Stephen. He was beyond terrified; he was screaming with it.

I'm in the dark. I'm in the dark. I'm in the dark. His litany was screaming in her head, and she had to block him for a moment. When she was calmer to hear him, she told him to shut up. His silence was almost as bad as his screams.

I'm going to get you. She looked around the room to see what she could do to get away, and saw the gun and the blade on the table. Edward had used them both on her after he'd gotten tired of his fists, but she'd never spoken to him or whimpered, no matter the pain he caused. *You have to be calm or I won't be able to talk to you.*

They've put me in the casket. I'm buried alive again. He was panting, his voice full of terror. She knew that he had a real fear of the darkness, and her heart broke for him. When she tried to talk to him again, he kept repeating the same thing over and over. *I'm in the dark.*

I would love to have you in the dark right now. She had to talk loudly so he'd hear her. *I'd do all manner of things to you if you were with me. First I'd start with your cock. Take it into my mouth.* He didn't seem to hear her, so she sent him images as he'd done to her one night not so long ago. Stephen told her to stop. Then he continued. Giving up for now, she reached for Samuel. His words were of very little comfort when he realized who it was.

Christ, where the hell are you? She tried to tell him she didn't know, but he continued before she could. *There was blood all over the front of the house, almost as if they'd taken buckets of your blood and thrown it at the place. Then the inside wasn't any better. Do you know who did this?*

Velvet December, the vamp from Stephen's past. My stepfather is here as well. He's been changed, but I think it's recent. She rolled her neck to feel the pull of his bites. *He bit me. Not badly, but enough that he's drained me just a little. And this bitch, Velvet, has a new level of crazy going for her. I'm going to hurt her up pretty badly when I get free.*

She waited for him to say something, and when he didn't, she told him about Stephen. *Yeah, I know. I tried to reach him because I could feel his fear, but it was too much. I'm sorry, but I don't know how to reach him when he's in this sort of state. Can you calm him?*

I've tried. She looked around the room. *We're in a house. I can see that someone has taken care of where we are. And I can smell laundry detergent and bleach. Strange I know, but I think we're in the basement, not the sub levels of a house.*

Good to know. I don't suppose you know if Stephen is in the same house as you. I've got my men out looking, but I don't have a clue where to start.

She told him she didn't know either. *I think Stephen was here, but not now. They've buried him somewhere.* She didn't tell him that was the cause of his crippling fear. Clar had no idea if Stephen had ever shared what had happened to him so very long ago, but she had a feeling that Samuel knew.

Vinnie said he's had his blood. He thinks he can find him faster than we can. She remembered that too and told Samuel that she agreed. Looking down at her chained arms, she realized that it was silver and frowned.

Shouldn't I have some sort of reaction to silver since Stephen changed me? I mean, something? He told her congratulations, and that silver was poison to her kind. *It's not bothering me. I mean, not even a tiny bit.*

Then what are you waiting for? Get out of that shit. She decided she wanted to punch him in the nose for acting as if it were no big deal. Then she felt another person trying to contact her and reached out to the person.

Hello, love. Are you in need of me? She didn't know who it was until he laughed. Vinnie. *Hawk and I are looking for Stephen, but if you need me to come there and get you, I can try and find you first.*

No, find him. She started to ask him if he knew where she was but decided that she was going to do this on her own. Pulling her arm straight up, she heard the steel chair give. *I'm going to take care of business here. You find Stephen for me. And Vinnie, you guys should be careful when you do. He's a little stressed right now.*

I know, love. We've exchanged blood. And while I don't understand why you and I have this connection, I can feel your fear for him as well. We'll take care. I've told Samuel where you are, but also cautioned him to stay back. I told him you were going to take this bitch out. She thanked him. *No problem. I would like to talk to you once this is over. There are a few things…okay, a great many things I'd like to ask you.*

Deal. She pulled over and over on the steel, holding her arms until it finally gave way. Freeing her other arm was easier when she could use both her arms' strength. When her legs were finally unlatched, she stood up, only to stagger back a little. She needed to eat.

Moving upwards instead of down where she knew the lair had to be, Clar searched through the house to find someone. She didn't know if she could drink from a stranger, but Stephen needed her and she had to find him now. The first person she encountered had her stepping back in the shadows. Clar had no idea why, but she could not bite the woman who walked just down the hall from her. Just as she was ready to give up because she couldn't make it work, another person walked by her, and she reached for him just as he moved past her.

As soon as she bit into him, she felt the rich taste of his blood and knew that he was a wolf. Drinking deeply, she looked up when something caught her eye. It was Leith, and she and a dozen or so other faeries from the house were hovering just in front of her. Clar lifted her head, hating what they'd caught her doing.

"It is necessary." Leith came toward her, but not close enough for her to touch her. "We have located the witch below. When you are ready, we will accompany you."

"You don't need to do that. I'd rather you helped Vinnie find Stephen."

Leith looked at the other with her and then back at her. Clar had a feeling she was going to tell her it was too late, and her heart ached with it.

"He is well. His lordship has help from the others. Master Vicente will have no trouble locating him now." Clar started to ask her what that meant, but the wolf struggled enough so that she remembered he was there. "Finish him."

She knew what Leith meant. Kill him. She wasn't one to go around murdering people simply because they pissed her off, and she shook her head. Another faerie came closer to her, and she could see his horror.

"He murdered a woman and her child today. And the day before, another. His tastes run toward the helpless. He chases them to have their blood spiked with fear. He is a monster of the same breed as the woman below." She nodded and looked at the man. Reaching into his mind, she saw that he'd not just killed over the past two days but all his life. Snapping his head around, she heard his neck break, and she dropped him to the ground.

The move to the sub levels was much easier than it had been for her to come up. The faeries made sure she went the right way and even showed her which door to open when they got downstairs. The woman certainly did like velvet, she thought.

The house wasn't just done up in velvet but seemed to be made of it. The walls were papered with a dark blood-colored design that made Clar slightly sick to see. The drapes were of the same color, but a solid wall of blood-like material that had her thinking of a bloodied waterfall. Even the furniture was of the same material, but fringed in gold so that it hung in long ponytail-like fingers from each chair or table. When they stood outside the room, Clar had a moment of worry when she smelled blood.

"'Tis the murderer." She looked at Leith, not sure she understood. "The man who harmed you all those years ago. While we are happy to have you as our queen, he did kill your mother, and for that I am glad he is dead."

Her stepfather. She didn't feel any remorse for his death other than the fact that she would dearly have loved to have done it, but she knew that however he'd died, it was much too quick for her taste. When she started to turn the knob, she felt Vinnie touch her mind.

"We've found him. And I'm sending Hawk for you. Whatever you're going to do there, hurry it along. He's over the deep end."

Opening the door, she smelled death immediately. Her mission had changed from making the vampire suffer to getting her dead so she could go to Stephen. But as soon as she was standing over the bed, she knew that she couldn't do it. Not like this. The woman had made too many people suffer at her hand.

"Call the council. Tell them to come for her." Leith nodded and smiled. "I'm not saying I don't want to kill her, but they've found Stephen and he's much more important."

"They are on their way. I shall wait for them. You must go to Master Hawk." Clar nodded and started for the door. As she opened it, Clar had a brief moment of fear when a shape moved toward her. But it was only a group of faeries. She looked at Leith.

"I am but small, my lady, and would not be able to hold her alone." Clar nodded but still didn't leave. "We will not be harmed by her. She will…cooperate, or she will never make it before the council."

The threat was there. It wasn't implied but promised. Clar wanted to tell her to be careful but was sure that it wasn't her that would be harmed if Velvet were to wake now. She could almost feel sorry for the vampire. Almost. But whatever happened was nothing short of what she deserved.

Chapter 12

Stephen knew that he needed something, but his mind would not focus on what or who it might have been. There were beings around him, and, try as he could, none of their faces looked familiar. When one of them took a step toward him, he lashed out before he could think not to.

"Stephen." The voice made his heart jump, but he wasn't sure if the person talking was someone he should kill or let live. "Listen to me. She's on her way. I swear to Christ, she's on her way."

Someone was coming. The women who had put him here? She was coming back, and he wasn't going back in that hole for any amount of money. Someone or a great many someone's were going to die if they tried. He lashed out again with his claws when someone came near again.

"What the fuck are you doing?' He stilled. The voice sounded…. "Are you out to scare the shit out of everyone or just to piss them off? Do you think we have nothing better to do with our time than to stand around and let you take swipes at us?"

"I'm not going back in that fucking hole. You try it again, bitch, and you'll be joining me." She laughed, and he took a step toward her. She didn't move. His eyes were so full of his beast that all he could see was her heat and nothing of the face that spoke to him.

"I wouldn't mind going in the dark with you. I told you that before." His mind grasped at something, but it was too fleeting for him to remember. "Did you enjoy the pictures I sent you?"

"Who is this?" He heard a man's voice but not what he was saying. "Who is with you? You're going to need more than one man to take me down, Velvet. I'm not going to go easily. I have a mate and I love her."

"Do you? Do you love me, Stephen?" She was talking softly, but he could hear her. Before he could ask her again who she was, she spoke again. "I can't tell you my name. They told me that you had to say it. It would bring you back to me."

"Bullshit. Tell me your name." Her laughter made him stand up straighter when a thought of that same laughter came at him from another time. She'd been in his yard with others. "Who are you?"

"Who am I? You know me. Concentrate on me. You have to remember or the beast won't let you go." His beast was protecting him, and he told her this. "He doesn't need to protect you from me. He likes me too."

"He likes no one." But he did. And the longer he stood there talking to the woman, the more he felt his beast want to curl into her. Stephen could see now too. There was still a bloodied circle around his vision for the most part, but he could make out shapes now. "Someone put us in a casket and buried us."

"I know. And when you had this hissy fit, I had to leave her to the faeries so I could come and calm you down. What do you suppose will happen to her once she is brought before the council? Do you think they'll bury her again? Or will they be less inclined to let someone unearth her again?" He felt his body moving toward the voice, the need for her to touch him great. "My stepfather is dead. When I left him, he was ash on the floor. It looked like she'd rammed a dagger in his chest and killed him."

"Velvet December." He heard the woman say yes but nothing more. "You're not her. She is the one that…my beast is only protecting me."

"I'm glad he is. Otherwise Vinnie would never have found you." He had called out, his beast had, and when he had, someone had answered him. "Vinnie said that the faeries helped him, and without their help, he might not have ever found you."

She was coming into focus now. He could make out her shape and that she was a vampire. He took a step toward her and was surprised when she took one to him. He would have thought she'd be afraid of him, but she stood her ground.

"I won't hurt you." She nodded and smiled. He looked at her face and was captured by her eyes, the startling blueness of them. "Samuel told me it was like looking into the ocean. Then he said it was like the oceans and the heavens both."

Stephen touched his fingers to her face and felt his claws retract. He wanted to touch her everywhere but was afraid of hurting her. He realized then that his fear was gone, the need for this woman overriding it. Stephen pulled her to his body, and she wrapped around him. He didn't just feel like she was his, but his universe.

"I'd like to take you to my bed." Her laughter made him smile, and he held her tighter. "I love you, Clarice. I would very much like for you to marry me."

"I'd like that as well, but we have to wait a few more days." He felt her hunger then and could smell the other vampire on her. Tilting her head, he could see the mark that someone else had given her, and he felt his beast rise again. "Don't let him go just yet."

"Someone dared to bite what is mine?" She nodded but held him to her. "I will kill them. Tell me who it was, now."

"It was my stepfather." Stephen knew that the man was lucky he was dead. What he'd had planned for him in the few seconds he'd figured out she'd been hurt was enough to tell him that he was still on the edge. Looking over her shoulder, he saw Vinnie there, as well as Hawk, both of whom he knew he owed so much.

"You're a lucky man." Stephen nodded at Vinnie. "And as much as I'd like to stand here and go over the finer things of having a woman that will put up with you, I can feel the pull of the faeries. I need to get back to them and calm them down."

"You've a special relationship with them." Vinnie only nodded and looked at Hawk. There too was a man who Stephen would give his life for. "I thank you for this. You could have hurt me, but you got her to me instead."

"Yeah, I don't want you to think that we did it for you. Had we hurt you in any way, I'm pretty sure she would have kicked our collective asses." Stephen laughed, and Clar glared at him. "You're not what I expected in a mate for him."

"You're not what I expected in a shifter, either." Stephen knew that Hawk wasn't just a normal shifter but much more. He'd also heard rumors that the man could speak to inanimate objects. He wondered if they were true, and decided that they were not only true but probably grossly undervalued too. When both men shifted and took to the sky, he looked at Clarice.

"Shall we go home? I have a powerful need to mark you again." Her body responded more quickly than he'd thought it would, her scent overwhelming his needy beast. "You're going to make him take you now."

"Promise?" Stephen growled and grabbed her hand. He was dragging her to the closest hard object when he was suddenly in his house. "Fuck me, Stephen. Mark me again, and then I need to mark you. Some fucking bitch got her scent all over you."

Taking her into his arms, he carried her to the bathroom. A shower was something they both needed. Her clothes were covered in blood, and he smelled of death. Stripping them both down, he turned on the water and lifted her onto the counter.

"I need a taste." She nodded and leaned back, lifting her breasts up. It wasn't what he'd had in mind, but they were too tempting to refuse. Taking her left breast into his mouth, he suckled on it while he pulled on the nipple of the other one until she was as hard as his cock.

"You're going to make me come." He growled at her and lifted his head. Picking her up by her ass, he took them under the spray. Stepping back from her, he reached above her head for the large sponge.

"I'm going to wash you." She nodded and stood still while he filled the sponge with soap. "And while I'm getting you clean, I'm going to nibble at every inch of you."

Her moan had his cock straining from his body. When her fingers wrapped around him, he closed his eyes. She slid up and down his shaft with her hand while he washed her breasts. Leaning down, he took her breast into his mouth again while she guided his cock to her pussy.

"I want you inside of me." He nodded, but she pushed him back first. His knees bumped into the small seat in the shower, and he sat down. She got down on her knees in front of him, taking the sponge from his limp fingers.

He nearly came when she rubbed the rough thing over his cock head. He watched her slide it up and down his shaft several times before she finally took him into her mouth. Stephen curled his fingers into her hair as he held her there, praying that he didn't come too soon, but knew that if he did, he'd be ready again in no time. This woman could do that to him.

The sponge moved over his balls, and he rolled his hips upward. When she swallowed, tightening her throat around him, Stephen felt his eyes roll to the back of his head. He wanted to come down her throat, but the need to mark her was too much. Lifting her from his cock, he whimpered when she licked the stream of his precum from her mouth.

"Stand up." She nodded and stood up. Stephen couldn't help but take a taste of her pussy and pulled her to him to take one. When he licked her clit, she cried out just as she flooded his mouth with cream. He drank from her as she rode his mouth over and over through her climax. Standing up, he pressed her to the shower wall and lifted her up again. Without waiting for her to wrap around him, he slammed his cock as deeply as he could and pounded hard.

"Come for me. Come so I can feed from your spiced blood." She tilted her head and nipped at his shoulder. As soon as she threw back her head and called his name, Stephen pulled her throat to him and bit her. Blood, spiked with her climax and her own special taste, had him coming too. His body exploded inside of her as he drank deeply. Sealing the wounds, he turned off the water and took her to the bedroom, not even bothering to grab a towel. There he dropped on top of her even as she touched the bed. This time he held her hands above her head while he bit into her breast.

Stephen knew that he was hurting her on some level. His beast needed to mark her as well, and he let him go. Her cries made him look down at her as he fucked her as hard as he could, and he saw her own beast rising from inside of her. When she flipped him to his back, he lay there, stunned by what he was seeing.

"She wants you." He nodded and started to move his hips. "No. She wants you. Let her please. I'm afraid she wants to take you."

Let her, his mind screamed. But before he could tell her, Clarice started riding him, her hips moving fast, her body swaying as she held herself steady with her hands curled in his chest. When she leaned back, her body bowed, Clarice cupped her breast with one hand and slid her fingers into her pussy with the other. He sat up and took her offered breast as he pulled her hips to him. Sliding his hand down her back to her ass, he found her tight rings and punched his two fingers into her. Clarice screamed her release, and he rolled her to her back and took her throat even as he emptied himself in her again.

Lying atop her, he lifted his head. He could feel her hunger now and felt bad for it. Tilting his head, Stephen offered her his throat and cried out when she took it. His cock, semi-hard before, hardened immediately. He moved in and out of her as she drank his life giving blood.

When she finished, he kissed her mouth and tasted his blood. Moaning, he rolled his hips harder. When she came this time, Stephen offered her his throat again, and wasn't surprised by her teeth grazing him but not biting. When she touched her tongue to his shoulder, he came the moment she sank her teeth into him and felt her join him. They were so exhausted that they fell asleep, still tangled around each other.

~~~

Kasen was in the kitchen when she made her way down the stairs. The man was forever in there now, and she wondered if he thought he should stay there in the event she was hungry. But he wasn't alone today. Samuel and Kennedy were with him. Clar got herself a glass of water and sat down with them. Stephen, she knew, was coming down as well.

"You're here to tell me something. Something I'm not going to like." Samuel nodded and looked at the doorway when Stephen walked in. She squeaked when he picked her up and sat her onto his lap.

"Tell us. I can feel you're upset about something. Just tell us so we can go back to bed." She flushed at Stephen's words, but no one seemed to notice. Kasen sat a plate of food in front of her, and that's when she noticed that it looked as if he'd cooked for the Payne's as well.

"The wolf that Clar killed? His pack leader is demanding that she be put to death. He said that he had permission to be there, and that she violated his rules as leader by killing one of his own without a trial." He handed them a picture of the man as a human. Clar thought Samuel was kidding, but with one look at Kennedy, she knew that he wasn't. "Unless she can prove she was being harmed in some way by the man, she has to either become his bitch or die by his hand."

"He killed a family two days before. And the morning before he took us from our home, he killed a mother and child." Samuel nodded as if he knew this too. "Can anything be done about that?"

"No. Not as far as the pack leader is concerned. He said the man was his second in command and that he was needed." Samuel looked at Kennedy, then at her before he continued. "I'm with you. He should have been killed a long time ago, but he is correct in saying that...wait, what did you say? He was here when you were taken?"

"Yes. He was the one who knocked me down. And he was the first person in the door, too. Also, when I was being tied up at the house, I came to just enough to see him there. He was the one holding the gun on me while this other man, another wolf, tied me up." He asked her if she was sure. "Yeah, I'm sure. There was a woman there too, in the house. When I came from the sub levels, I saw her first. But for some reason I couldn't touch her. She was...I guess undesirable."

"She was breeding. And she was there when I was taken too. I could smell her and was surprised that they'd bring a breeding female on a raid." Stephen looked at her. "You can never feed from a pregnant woman. I know that there are books saying that we do that, but something in their DNA will poison us if we try."

Clar nodded, understanding now. Kennedy got up and opened the door. Both she and Stephen stood up when a man, a wolf, came to the step but stopped. Clar reached out and held the man there while Stephen spoke to Samuel. This man was the one who had chained her to the chair.

"He was here as well." Samuel stood up and put Kennedy behind him as he watched the man. Stephen stepped in front of them and continued. "He can't move. Clar has him and he's not strong enough to break it. It's the same kind of shield she used on the mountain that day."

The room suddenly filled. Kasen moved toward her, but she held him back with a lifting of her hand. She didn't want anyone hurt, but there would be a massive body count if anyone touched what was hers. The first man to approach her nearly got to be number one when Stephen stepped in front of her.

"Don't touch my mate." The man nodded and backed up. "She will speak to you, but you have no reason to touch her."

"I understand." The stranger smiled at her as he spoke. "My name is Kent. I am the Lord of Garston. Do you know of me?"

"Nope." He nodded, and she watched him fight a smile. "You think I should have? 'Cause I got to tell you right now, I'm not too thrilled with the last visitor we had today."

"I am the man who would be your boss." She shook her head. "You do not believe me? I assure you that I —"

"I don't have a boss. Nor do I want one. If this has to do with me being a vampire, then, okay, I'll listen to you. But don't expect me to bow down at your feet. I've had enough bowing and scraping, thanks." He looked at Stephen, then at her again. "You can ask him. I don't really do what he tells me either."

"She is more like you than I would have hoped." Clar smiled, loving the compliment. "It was not meant to be something you should be proud of. Yet I do believe you are."

"I am. Not that I give two nuts about your opinion of me and what I do. What the hell are you doing here now?" He pointed to the wolf. "He's yours? You should teach your puppies to have better manners."

"He belongs to me." The second man stepped forward, but unlike the first one, didn't try to touch her. "I'm Marsh. I too am on the council. We have...the puppy, as you called him, came to us complaining about your treatment of his pack. We only came to investigate."

"No you didn't." Clar looked at Stephen when he snapped. "You came here to bring me to heel. Well, it won't work. I'm not going to join the council."

Clar had had enough. She moved forward a step and put a hand on both men. When the wolf staggered back, she gripped his arm and held him until she was finished. As soon as she'd given them all the information she'd taken from the wolves at the house, she stepped back. When Stephen wrapped his arms around her, she leaned into him. She didn't want these idiots to know how weak it had made her.

"You're hungry. I'll take care of you when they leave." She moaned at him, and he leaned into her throat and nipped at her. "Behave or this will take longer than is necessary. I will take you up to bed now and they'll wait on us. Or we can finish this and they'll all leave."

"What you have done…you gave me…it is theirs?" Kent staggered to the chair and sat down. Marsh was already there, staring at the man she still held in the bubble. "You have given us their memories so that…do you know what people would do for that kind of power?"

"Yeah, I do." She put out her hand, and he backed away from her. "But if I were you, I'd be more worried about what I got when I touched you. What you should be doing is this…simply forget what you know about me and deal with the wolf."

"He has been murdering humans for a long time." Clar almost felt sorry for Marsh. He looked as if he'd been told there was no more chocolate. And that just wasn't something she wanted to hear either. He looked at her. "I've no doubt that what you've given me is true, but I simply don't…what am I to do with the information? How can I justify his death and the dealing with his pack without the physical truth?"

"The woman…I think her name was Julie. She will talk to you. The child she carries is her mate's, who was killed by this bastard. Had she been showing when he took her in, he would have simply killed it within her womb. His plan now is to kill the child the moment it is born. She was with them when things went down. Ask her." When Marsh stood up, he nodded and then looked at Stephen. With another nod, he came to her and put out his hand.

"Is there a way to thank you and only get a handshake?" She smiled at his laughter and put out her hand. As soon as she touched him, she gave him a little more information. He looked shocked but said nothing as he turned to Kent. "We should leave these people to their lives. I think Stephen has told us enough times that he is not going to join forces with us."

"You can't be serious. You're going to simply let them walk away, after everything we've found out about her? No, I demand that we bring them in or tell the world what we know." Kent looked at her as he continued. "With a power like yours, I can rule the world of vampires."

Marsh shifted in seconds, and leapt at the other vampire just as Clar shoved Stephen back into Samuel, and they both hit the floor. The man in the doorway was knocked out of his hold, but he also hit his head and lay there while the big wolf tore out the throat of Kent. It was over in seconds. He stood there panting as he watched them all.

"He was going to kill all of you." Everyone looked at her as she spoke. "I saw it in his mind and told Marsh. He was going to kill him and blame it on this house, then take me away with him to keep under lock and key. I've been…he kills people who would be stronger than him. His plan was to get Stephen to join the council then have him murdered. He found that…he thought that Stephen was a threat to him."

"You got all that from a touch?" She looked at Samuel when he asked. Shaking her head he looked at Stephen. "You told her."

"No. She can read minds. So can I." Samuel started to speak, then sat down as Stephen continued. "You knew that she could. Why are you surprised?"

"I guess I figured that when you converted her that she'd lose some of that ability. I have no idea why when every other female in this group has gotten stronger." Samuel rubbed his hand over his face and stared at her. "You know what I'm thinking right now?"

"Yeah," she told him with a grin. "You're thinking you and the rest of these people are going to get the hell out of here so I can go upstairs and have all kinds of monkey sex with my mate."

"Christ." Samuel got up and looked at her before he smiled. "Welcome to the family. And so you know, you scare the shit out of me."

"Good." Ten minutes later, Jimmy and a few of his pack came to collect the wolf. Marsh walked out the door with him, and Clar knew the moment he asked Jimmy to run the other pack. Jimmy wasn't going to go easy either. He loved where he was now. Clar turned to Kasen when he cleared his throat.

"There will only be the two of you for dinner?" She smiled at him, and he laughed. "I see. Would you mind much if I were to take my missus out? It has been a long while since we've had a date."

She was moving up the stairs with Stephen when she realized what he'd said. "Kasen is married?"

Chapter 13

Stephen moved through the house without touching the floor. He knew that someone was there and didn't want them to know just yet he was aware of them. As soon as he entered the living room, he knew who it was and leaned against the door to watch the man. Hawk didn't turn as he spoke.

"I know you are aware of my affinity to inanimate objects." Stephen told him he was. "Sometimes they call to me. It's mostly vehicles or something of that nature. But there are times when something like a piece of furniture does. Your desk, do you know where you got it?"

"It came with the house. Along with the bookshelf to your right and wingback by the fireplace." Hawk nodded and moved to the chair he told him about. He was running his hand along the back of it when he frowned.

"Your mate, did you know that she can do this as well? You too, I would imagine." Stephen didn't answer because he was pretty sure that Hawk wasn't really talking to tell him anything, but working up to something. "This chair was original to the house. The desk came from elsewhere before being brought here. It has some stories it would like to be told. A problem to be solved."

He walked to the shelf and put his hand on the trim that ran along the top. When he pushed one of the ornate flowers in, a large section of the trim popped out. He handed the drawer like piece to him.

"It's a will." Hawk went back to the desk and pressed on the scroll work across the visitor side of the desk and another drawer, this one much larger, slid from under the desk near the leg. This he handed to him as well. In this one was a large leather pouch and a leather-bound notebook.

Stephen opened the will and read it quickly before taking out the pouch. He couldn't believe how heavy it was and laid it on the desk with a thud. The leather-bound notebook was heavy as well, and he opened it first. He started laughing the moment he realized what he was reading.

"It's a letter to the finder. It says that whoever finds this is a treasure all of their own. I think it was a teenager. And by the prose, I'd say from the fourteenth century." Hawk touched the pouch, then nodded. Stephen continued telling the story as he read.

"He was sixteen and sickly. His father was a merchant sailor and died at sea. The mother had to sell everything they owned to keep from going to debtors' prison. Apparently his plan was to find the desk when they were settled and get his treasures. He goes on to say how his father was a bastard and that he was glad to be rid of him." Stephen picked up the pouch and dumped it on the desk. "Christ."

"He was a pick-pocket." Clar spoke as she came into the room and smiled at Hawk. "Hello. I thought you'd be back."

Stephen looked at his friend and lifted a brow. Hawk flushed and stammered a little before he explained. He was embarrassed, something Stephen would never had guess the man to ever be.

"I was just telling Stephen you could do this as well." She sat down next to him and picked up the biggest emerald he'd ever seen. She put it down and picked up the dozen or so rubies that lay in the pile and started to separate them by gem as Hawk continued. "The boy is hanging around the desk. He wants someone to…he has descendants. Not many, but they could use this money. He doesn't want them to have it all because he believes they will spend it stupidly, but he does want to know if you'll help them."

"Yes." Stephen looked at Clar when she spoke. "If you don't mind, I guess. It's your desk after all."

"It's our desk and yes, we'll help them out." He picked up the will and handed it to her. "This is not from the same kid. This was put in years later and is written by hand. I'm sure that whoever put it there hoped that someone would find it after he passed."

"His lover died before him. They were together when they were robbed." She put the will down and looked at him. "The son killed them for the money. He decided that since they had cut him off without a penny, he'd take it all. He still lives and has worked his way through their savings and is now looking for a way to capitalize on more."

Stephen waited. There was something else going on here. Something that had Hawk come into their home in the middle of the night. When he started to help Clar separate the gems out, Stephen nearly told him to get to it when he finally spoke.

"I have found something…someone. She's just a child, but she is haunted by something that I cannot touch. I was wondering if you'd help me." He didn't look up from what he was doing but continued speaking in low tones. "Her parents despair of her ever being normal...not that I really know what normal is, but she won't be unless the thing that haunts her is dealt with."

"A spirit?" Hawk shrugged at Clar. "You don't know what it is or you don't want to tell us?"

"You, not both of you. While Stephen is as strong as you are, he is a male. And the spirit that harms her is male." Before Stephen could point out that he was male, Hawk explained. "I come to her as my hawk. For some reason we can speak, even though there is no reason for us to be able to."

"You think she's a clairvoyant like me." Again he shrugged. "Do you know anything? I mean, so far all we know is she's a kid who's having nightmares."

"He is killing her." Hawk got up to pace. "This thing doesn't just haunt her, but he takes her body. And when he does, he makes her harm herself. Not like that movie where the little girl was possessed by the devil, but a spirit. I think he might be a ghost that has found himself a toy. Two times I've been there when he's taken her over. He will do things like try to drown her in the tub. Once he had her leap from a tall building, and if not for the man below, she would have fallen to her death."

"You think he's doing this to kill her so he has a playmate?" Hawk turned to look at Clar. Stephen could see by the look on his face he'd not considered that. When he sat down, he looked pale and afraid.

"He could, couldn't he? Kill her so that her spirit will be there for him forever." Clar stood up and so did he. "You will help me?"

"Now. We'll go now." They both disappeared, leaving Stephen there alone. It took him several seconds to realize that he had no idea where they'd even gone. Standing up, he started putting the gems in the pouch again when Hawk came back. He was grinning.

"I got caught up in the moment." Stephen nodded. "Would you like to come with us? I'm not sure what you can do for her, but if you'd like to come I can—"

"Protect her." Hawk nodded. "Make sure that whatever happens there that you protect her at all costs. And I will take care of the other things."

"You're a good man." Stephen shook his head. "You are. I was worried you'd tell me no. That you'd say something about mates and that she wasn't going to be allowed to help me."

"Have you met my mate? I mean, seriously, do you think if I tried to tell her she could or couldn't do anything, it would go over all that well? I think she'd simply do whatever I said she couldn't just to piss me off." He smiled at Hawk. "You'll have a mate that will—"

"No. I can't. I don't...I know that most men our age would say that we're too set in our ways, that finding a mate this late in our lives is going to be difficult or some shit like that. But I never want a mate because of what I am. A woman would be...she wouldn't be able to understand what I am."

"You'd be surprised." Hawk only shook his head and told him he'd watch over Clarice. "See that you do. And let me know if you or she needs me."

After he was gone, Stephen wandered about the house. He used to do this before he'd found Clarice...move from room to room and enjoy the peace and quiet of it all. Now the silence bothered him. It was entirely too...well, there was no Clarice there to make it a home. Finally he settled at the desk again and read the will. His first order of business was to find this family, then deal with the gems for the young man.

~~~

Clar watched the little girl interact with Hawk. She was so gentle with him that she wanted to sit and watch them for hours. But when she turned to look at Clar, she could see the hatred there as well as something evil.

"You think you have me figured out?" The voice of the small child was so contrary to the harshness of the words. Clar didn't say anything as the child/thing laughed. "I'm not going to leave her be. And even if you do manage to get me to leave her, I'll just find someone else to play with."

"You think?" Clar sat down and pretended to consider his words. "Nah, I don't think that's going to happen. You see, I'm a good deal stronger than you are, and not to mention, I know what you're up to."

"Do not." When he moved from the girl and sat on the bed beside her, she could see what had happened to him.

"There was a fire. And you were left behind." Clar knew the kid from his picture in the paper the previous year. The fire and the deaths had made the headlines for months. Petey glared at her, and she hurt for him. "You started the fire, but you in no way killed you and your two sisters. The fire you set burned down the entire building."

"So." He got up to walk to the window, and she wondered if he could see out without Daniy, the little girl's body. "I can start a fire here too if I want. Do you think she'll be able to find her way out of here without me?"

"I think you'd mislead her just so she would die." He looked at her, and she could see she'd hit a nerve. "Is that what happened with your sisters? You tried to get them out and got all turned around?"

186

"I told you I set the fire. What more do you want from me? You think I got them lost in the building to make them die with me? I wasn't going to be the only dead person. I wanted company." He moved toward her, and she noticed that he moved through the bed and not around it. "I killed them."

"No, you didn't." He stopped moving. "You might have set the fire, but it wasn't to kill anyone. It was to keep them warm. You also did try to get them out, but unfortunately for you and your sisters, your mother locked you in the house so that she could go to a friend's house to get high. There was no way you could have gotten them out."

"She said she'd be back soon and that we'd be okay." He looked at Daniy when she started to cry. "I didn't make her do that."

"Of course you didn't. You're scaring her though. She's as frightened as your sisters were when your mother locked the door. How long were you in there?" He looked at Daniy again and reached out to smooth her hair. She couldn't see him, Clar thought, but she could feel his touch. "Your name is Petey, right? Your sisters were Porsche and Grace."

"They were little. Both of them were so little. I couldn't carry them at the same time." He looked at her. "Mom put a box of diapers in the room with us and a box of cereal with some milk. There wasn't enough milk for their bottles and the food, so I'd eat it dry to save them some. We were in there for a long time."

Clar knew how long they'd been left. The mother had claimed that she'd left them for only a weekend. But under further investigations it had been more like two weeks. It was a small wonder that they'd been able to survive as long as they had. The heat had been turned off the day after she'd left them, and the temperatures had dropped to below zero for nearly that entire week before they'd been murdered. The pictures in the paper of the fire had made her sad when she'd seen their lovely faces. The girls, a set of identical twins, were only seven months old; the little boy was six.

"You can't hurt her any more. Daniy's parents are very worried about her. You don't want her to die, do you?" He shook his head. "I can understand that you're lonely. I'm that way too, but she can be your friend. She can talk to you."

"I want her to play with me." Clar nodded and picked up a book. Daniy took it from her and turned to the first page and started reading. In a few minutes Petey sat beside her and looked at the pages as she turned them. "I didn't know she could read."

"I'm sure there are a good many things you don't know about her. Did you know that she has a brother? And that he has toys that he lets his sister play with? Maybe she could bring some in here for you and let you play with them." He looked at the floor that was covered in toys that Clar was sure he'd tossed there. "You'll have to be nicer to her or she'll cry again. Her parents might even move away, and then what will you do?"

"I don't want her to leave me." The temper flared again, and Daniy pulled away from him. Before Clar could tell him to calm, Petey touched the book again. "Tell her...can you tell her I'm sorry?"

"She knows." Daniy started reading the book again, but she kept looking in the direction where Petey was sitting. It wasn't long before Petey was smiling and laughing when the little girl did. Clar stood up.

"Are you leaving me?" She nodded at Petey. "Are you taking the man with you? The bird I mean?"

"I am. His name is Hawk. He's the one who brought me here." Petey nodded. "You're going to not hurt her now, right?"

"I won't hurt her." He looked longingly at the window. "I wish I could tell them I'm sorry. I didn't mean for them to die. And sometimes...I wish I could ask my mom why she didn't come back when she said she would."

She could have told him that she was in jail for their murders, but Clar doubted that would help him. Clar also thought about telling him that the little girls had died in his arms and that people around the world had been horrified by what had happened to them. That many sent money to pay for their funerals and the beautiful headstones that marked their tiny graves. But again, she didn't. It would do him little good now. Instead, she put out her hand and told him to take it. When he smiled at her, she knew that he'd made a connection with her.

"All you need to do is call out to me and I'll come to you. It might not be right away but I'll come, okay? You be a good boy and Daniy will care for you." He nodded. "I'm sorry that this happened to you, but you have a chance to be happy. Let it come to you."

She left with Hawk, and when she was alone in the living room, she went to find Stephen. He was on the phone with someone, so she sat in the chair across from him. When he hung up, she smiled at him.

"Would you like to have a baby?" He cocked a brow at her, and she laughed. "A real one, not a ghost."

"I don't know the first thing about kids. It's been...even holding Samuel's baby terrifies me to no end." He leaned back in the chair. "I would like to see you large with our child. The thought of you having my baby appeals to me."

"I think you're keener about making one than having one." He wiggled his brows at her. "What did you find out about the will and gems?"

"The family is in dire straits, but nothing that they couldn't have avoided. The young man came by. I had no idea that I could talk to the dead. Kind of scared me a little more than I thought it would. Anyway, he came by and asked me to give them only enough to pay the rent and their power bills. I told him that there was enough here to purchase a house and they'd never have to work again. Do you know what he said about that?"

"He said that they needed to work for what they wanted, not to have it handed to them. I think I like your ghost." Stephen growled, and she laughed. "Mine was a small boy who had been killed by neglect. At least your guy died of natural causes."

They both sat in silence, she was thinking about the young boy, and he more than likely was thinking about sex. She grinned. She stood up and sat on his lap.

"Tomorrow is the trial for Velvet. What do you suppose will come of it?" He pulled her closer to him and didn't say anything for a long time. Clar closed her eyes and was drifting off when he finally did speak.

"I'm going to propose that she be beheaded. We cannot take the chance on her being set free again. If she does, there will be no telling how much worse she will be." Clar agreed with him. "It'll have to be done by her accuser."

Clar sat up and looked at him. "You? You'll have to take her head off? It's not an easy thing to do. Not even if the person is someone you don't know. But you have a history with her. How do you feel about it?"

"I'm...I was going to say fine, but that makes me sound like a prick. And since I've met you, I'm not feeling so prick-like." He sat her on the desk and pulled his chair to her, positioning himself between her legs. "But I don't want to think about her right now. What I want to do is have a feast and you as the main course."

She leaned back and watched him as he pulled off her shoes and socks. She'd never have believed that it could be thought of as sexy when a man took them off for you. Her pants were next as he slowly peeled them from her body. He massaged her foot as he kissed her knees.

"Do you have any idea how much I love the taste of you? Not just your blood or even your luscious pussy, but your skin. It tastes like what I believe heaven to be like." He moved his mouth along the back of her knee by lifting her leg up. "And your taste gets stronger when you're aroused."

"You're making me crazy with need." He laughed softly as he pulled her to the edge of the desk and tore her shirt open from hem to neck. "Stephen, the moment you touch me with your mouth, I'm going to come."

"Good." He licked her thigh now, his tongue making a wet path to where she needed him most. When he opened her legs wider, she held her breath, knowing that she was going to need it when she screamed. "Come for me, baby. Come for me and let me drink my fill of you before I take you."

All she could manage was a nod as her panties were torn from her hips. When he lifted her up, pulling the last of the skimpy material from beneath her, she screamed when he licked her clit. Nothing could have stopped her from coming even if he'd held a gun to her head.

He ate her. Not just her clit, but her lips and thighs. Every time he touched his fangs to her skin, she cried out. When his tongue sealed the tiny wounds she knew he was giving her, she begged him for more. Clar wasn't sure how much more she could take when he stood up and opened his pants.

"I'm going to fuck you." She nodded and reached for his cock when he freed it, but he told her no. "If you touch me, even with your fingers, I'm going to come all over you, and I so desperately want to be buried deep inside of you. Lean back."

Her body was spread out for him, her legs wide on either side of his hips, her breasts bare of anything but her hands. Lifting and squeezing at them, she watched as he leaned over her, his cock at her entrance.

"Don't hold back." She told him that she couldn't anyway. "I'm not going to last long, and I want you to have as much pleasure as you can get."

His cock didn't just fill her but became a part of her. When he rolled his hips into her again and again, she felt her climax pull at her. And when he touched that part of her that made her scream, she did so, crying out his name over and over as he came with her. As soon as his teeth sank into her throat, Clar cried out and felt her world tilt off its axis. Too much, her mind told her just as blackness took her.

Chapter 14

Stephen watched the council. They were still upset with him because he'd not taken the position of leader, but now Marsh was on his side and things went a good deal better. They still wanted him, but now he had an ally. Stephen looked at Clar when she reached for his hand.

"What's taking them so long? I would have thought this thing would have started by now. Didn't they say it was to begin at ten sharp?" He laughed when she looked at her watch again. "It's ten after now. What the fuck are they waiting for?"

"Ten sharp to a vampire or any of these beings could be tomorrow." She looked at him aghast. "I'm kidding. They have to wait on the third. Since the death of one of their members they need an odd number to make sure that they don't have a tied vote."

He was sure that they were having a very hard time convincing anyone to reign on this council. Just an hour ago the person they had chosen decided that it would take up too much of his time, and Samuel had enough to do right now. Stephen laughed. He was sure that Kennedy had had a great deal to do with his decision. She hated the time he spent away from home now.

The doors behind him opened and they all stood up. The third had been found apparently, and when she came through the doors, Stephen burst out laughing. Samuel, however, was not amused.

Samuel's mother stood proud and glared at him when he laughed again when she looked his way. This was just too much for him, and he thought he was going to have to leave the room or be fined heavily. The council didn't like it when their panel was made fun of. When they were all seated, Summer stood up.

"As you know, there has been an opening on the council for many months now. Today, after much deliberation, I have taken on the role as head councilwoman for the paranormal. As of today, myself and the other council members, Marsh Dickerson and Penny Blackford, will preside over every case. We will also start on making the rules governing us more up-to-date, as well as fair to the ones we serve." She looked around the room, taking a deep breath. Stephen could see what this was costing her; she was as scared as he'd ever seen the woman. "Please bring in Sally Shunt, otherwise known as one Velvet December."

Her entrance could only be described as overdone. Much like most of her life, Velvet looked like what every human would ever think of a vampire as being, with a long, blood-red cape over a black skin-tight dress that displayed more of her than was strictly necessary. Her heels, when they could be seen under her lace, were pointed and covered in spikes. Stephen had a moment to wonder what Clarice would look like in such a pair. Then Velvet turned toward him.

"Christ." She had made her face up in a way that was both sad and hysterically funny. Dark lines circled her eyes so that she looked sultry and sexy. Her lips were covered in the reddest color he'd ever seen; he was not even sure that he could name it, it was so red. Rouge streaked across her cheeks, making her pale skin look all the whiter, and her nose was pierced several times with small diamond like studs.

The jewelry around her neck was a gold chain that had small vials hanging from it that he thought looked like they were blood filled. Her ears had hanging orbs dangling from them that at first glance he thought were swords, but were crosses. Each one was slightly different from the others. A total of about two dozen hung from each ear. He might have laughed if he wasn't afraid he'd never be able to stop. He wondered what she had been thinking when she'd gotten ready for this.

"She thinks she's scarier." He looked at Clarice when she whispered in his mind. "It's sad really, but she thinks that other than a slap on the wrist, they're going to tell her what she'd done was all right and let her go. She thinks they cannot put her to ground again."

"They can't." She looked at him when he answered her. "Once you are tried for a crime and the sentence is carried out, the same punishment cannot be applied. If it didn't work the first time, the council seemed to think that it was meant to be or some bullshit."

"You're kidding." He told her he wasn't. "Well, that just sucks the big one. Then what the hell are they going to do to her now? I was talking to a group of people before I came in here, and they said that the council said that they were too humane to murder their own kind. Is that true?"

"It was. I'm not sure about this group. Summer is a wonderful person and the kindest woman I've ever met before you. Do I think she can carry out justice on this kind of crime? I'm not so sure." They were asked to stand when the crimes against Velvet were read. They were longer than he'd thought, and listed among them were the death of fifty-three of her own children, humans she'd made into vampires then killed. Edward Barron was the last name to be read. Velvet was given a chance to respond to the list brought before her.

"You think anyone cares that a few people are dead? I don't." She snorted. "As a matter of fact, some of those people were worse than me. And when you think about it, I did us all a favor by taking them out. As for the others, I don't even remember doing that, so I want it taken from the list. I think it unfair that you even bring some of that shit up."

"How do you think the families of your victims feel about you being so cavalier about their deaths?" Velvet waved Summer off, and she continued. "What do you think people will say when we sentence you?"

"Sentence me? For what? Killing a few people that were going to die anyway? For doing what we all should be doing?" She shook her head as if she couldn't believe it was even a problem. "Get over yourself. Everyone knows that vampires kill. It's what we do best."

"I see. And the kidnapping of Stephen Silva and his mate, Clarice Kelley, what do you have to say about that?" Velvet looked at him and Clarice when Summer asked her. Stephen was sure if she hadn't been chained down, she would have leapt at them both. Instead, she just looked at Summer and answered her question.

"Stephen was mine before he got it into his head to take a mate. I should have been with him instead of this fucking human turned paltry vampire. She might look good on his arm, but he has to see what I can do with myself when we're together and know he's made a mistake." Velvet stood up and ran her hands down her body as she turned toward him. "See this? This is all yours when this trial is over."

"And what of his mate? What do you plan to do with her? I'm sure you've thought this out?" Velvet nodded at Summer and smiled at him again. Stephen felt his skin crawl when he thought that at one time she was his.

"I'm going to get rid of her, of course." Summer asked her what that meant. "Whatever it takes. I would have taken her out before, but she got away. And don't even try to pin that shit on me, either. I know the rules and rights of mates. He was mine."

"But not your mate." Velvet shrugged, but she did look decidedly more uncomfortable. "You would kill her to take her place in a man's life that has no use for you. How on earth do you think that would work? Mates are forever, and the love between them stronger than any bond. How did you think to conquer that?"

"Magic. I don't have that kind right now, but I have a deal with a mage. He said he could get it for me for a price." She looked at him and smiled. "You'd give me the money, won't you, love? I mean, it would be for a good cause?"

"You're fucking nuts." No one spoke when Clarice stood up and between him and Velvet. "You're one sick fucking cunt if you think for one minute I'm going to let you go near him, much less try to fuck him. He's mine and I love him."

Stephen was too stunned to say anything. She loved him was all he could think about. But when Velvet stood up and tried to break free of the bonds that held her, he did stand. Stephen put out his hand and a burst of power slipped from him to Velvet. She froze in mid curse.

The room seemed to have become empty of anyone, it was so silent. He looked up at Summer to see her staring at

him. He'd not meant to do anything more than just tell
Velvet to stop, but his beast and his newly found magic had
another idea.

"You all right?" He nodded at Summer and her
question. "Good. And since we have enough evidence now
to commence with the trial, I was wondering if you could let
her go."

He was wondering the same thing when Clarice put her
hand over his. The power still pouring from his hand
dissipated, and he felt the binding around Velvet let go. She
finished her cursing and sat down. He thought she looked
confused. Well, so was he.

"Sally Shunt, you are hereby s—"

"No, no, no. I'm Velvet. Say it. I want to hear you say
my name with you setting me free. Say it. Velvet December,
you are hereby set free." She laughed when Summer cocked
a brow at her. "You know you hate to say it, but you have
to. I've been tried once. You can try me all you want, but
you can't put me below the ground. I know my rights."

"You're correct, we can't. And that, thanks to you, is
going to be one of the first things I change. I can't sentence
you to the same punishment. That's why we've decided to
have you beheaded." Stephen watched Velvet and knew just
when what Summer had said sank in. She stood up so
quickly that two of the guards with her stepped back and
drew their weapons.

"You fucking bitch, you can't do that. I'm not an animal
that needs to be put down. You take that back right fucking
now." Summer nodded once and the guards took her arms
into their hands. "You tell them to let me go. I'm going to
hurt you when they do. I might even kill you, but you
cannot let them take my head off."

Stephen stood up when he was approached by one of the guards. He was handed the sword that he'd just recently had hung above the mantle in his office, the one that Jared had tried to kill him with all those weeks ago. Taking a step toward Velvet, he stopped when Samuel stood in front of him.

"I'll do it." He shook his head. "No. I want to do this. And I asked Mom and she said that as your leader I can take this for you. I want to. You're too invested in this and might hesitate. I'll make it a clean cut."

Stephen looked at Kennedy, then at his friend. There was love there along with the friendship they had, and he handed him the sword but kept his hand on the pommel. Samuel nodded once and took it from him. Stephen took Clarice into his arms and turned his back on Velvet. When her screams were abruptly cut off, he stood there holding Clarice until someone touched his shoulder.

"It's done." No one said anything to them as he and Clarice left the room. It was time for them to move on, and they'd have a much better chance at it now that there was no longer a threat hanging over them. Over either of them.

~~~

"So now what?"

Clar looked up when Stephen came into the dining room where she was working on something for Hawk. She laid her pen down and looked at him, trying to think about what he meant.

"What are you asking me? If it's about the house, I don't care. I'd like the extra room, but I can make do here." He sat in the chair, and she laughed at his expression. "You knew that I didn't care a fig for things like that when you met me. I was living in a cave, remember?"

"Yes I do, and if I also remember correctly, you had it organized as well." She looked at the table that she'd been using. It was covered in neatly laid out files, and if he thought to look at them, he'd see they were in alphabetical order as well. Her pens were laid out straight as well as the stack of empty files, and the label maker was filled and ready to continue with what she'd been doing.

"He called, you know. Hawk wanted to know if you were okay with what he'd asked you to do." Clarice picked up the pen she'd been using and set it back down. She didn't really know how to answer that. "I told him that I thought you were enjoying working with him."

"I am. I'm very..." She picked up the file she'd been working on and handed it to him. She knew the file like the back of her hand. "The man has been dead for nearly seventy years, and he's upset that his family has no idea that he'd had a will and that if they'd simply listened to him, things would be the way he wanted them to be. He's pissed at them. But it won't be better. He didn't leave any of them a thing, and had left his money to some charity that has been debunked for more years than I've been around. They divided the money up between them and used it to better themselves as well as their future families."

"And what are you going to do with the information?" She knew what she wanted to do with it, but she and Hawk had to talk about it first. She wanted to chuck the information she'd found and tell him to grow up. He was a tight-assed prick. "Clarice?"

"Hawk will decide. I get to put my input in, but he decides." She looked at him when he laughed. "You don't think I should be doing this, do you?"

"On the contrary, I think it's wonderful. I do wish that you'd keep your ghosties out of my office when I'm working. It's very distracting trying to close a business deal when one of them is screaming at me to make you mind." She laughed. "But the real reason I'm here is because I've got an answer about the house we looked at."

She held her breath. Clar really wanted the house, but was afraid it was too much for them. The house alone had more rooms than she knew she'd need. Then there was the yard and the wooded area behind the pool house. And then there was the... "Well?"

"We can move in as soon as you want." She screamed and went to him. Kissing him all over his face, he pulled her into his lap. "We'll have to get more furniture, of course, and then there will be a staff to hire. You'll also need to get a secretary, as I have suggested for you to do."

"I will. And I've been talking with Kasen and Nova. They said that they knew of a few people that we can hire right away." Clar thought of Nova, Kasen's wife, and was glad that they had gotten along so well. "Oh, and we'll need to give us separate offices. I want mine done all in white."

"Of course you do." He stood up with her in his arms and carried her to the stairs. "I was thinking we'd make love in celebration. And then we should go to our house and break it in as well. Perhaps if you're up to it, we can see if making love in the barn is all it's said to be."

"Stephen?" He stopped moving and looked down at her. "I love you. Very much."

"And I do you. But don't interrupt me. I'm making a list of places we need to break in. There are the ten bedrooms that we should furnish too. As well as the lair. We could have those properly broken in even before the first guest arrives."

She wrapped her arms around his neck and leaned into him. Clar was as happy as she'd ever been, and knew that for as long as they lived—and that was going to be a very long time—he'd make her smile.

About the Author

Kathi Barton, author of the bestselling series Force of Nature, lives in Nashport, Ohio with her husband Paul. In addition to writing full time Kathi likes to spend time with her eight grandkids, three children and three children-in-laws. She writes to relax and have fun.

Her muse, a cross between Jimmy Stewart and Hugh Jackman brings them to life for her readers in a way that has them coming back time and again for more. Her favorite genre is paranormal romance with a great deal of spice. You can visit Kathi on line and drop her an email if you'd like. She loves hearing from her fans. aaronskiss@gmail.com.

Follow Kathi on her blog:
http://kathisbartonauthor.blogspot.com/

PRAISE FOR THE DEAD COLD SERIES

Here are some of the over 100,000 five star reviews left for the Dead Cold Mystery series.

"Rex Stout and Michael Connelly have spawned a protege."

AMAZON REVIEW

"So begins one damned fine read."

AMAZON REVIEW

"Mystery that's more brain than brawn."

AMAZON REVIEW

"I read so many of this genre...and ever so often I strike gold!"

AMAZON REVIEW

"This book is filled with action, intrigue, espionage, and everything else lovers of a good thriller want."

AMAZON REVIEW